"I'm planning to get married."

For perhaps three seconds Tully didn't move, just sat staring at her, his expression a total blank.

Then he moved like an explosion, scraping his chair away from the table so it screeched on the floor and the jacket hanging over the back swung violently. *"You're what?"*

Looking at him looming over her, Lacey blinked. "I'm getting married," she repeated.

His eyes looked black and brilliant, fixing intently on her. "So..." he said. "Who's the lucky man?"

FROM HERE TO PATERNITY—romances that feature fantastic men who *eventually* make fabulous fathers. Some seek paternity, some have it thrust upon them, all will make it—whether they like it or not!

DAPHNE CLAIR lives in Aotearoa, New Zealand, with her Dutch-born husband. Their five children have left home but drift back at irregular intervals. At eight years old she embarked on her first novel about taming a tiger. This epic never reached a publisher, but metamorphosed male tigers still prowl the pages of her romance novels. Her other writing includes nonfiction, poetry and short stories, and she has won literary prizes in New Zealand and America. Daphne Clair also writes as Laurey Bright.

Don't miss any of our special offers. Write to us at the following address for information on our newest releases.

Harlequin Reader Service
U.S.: 3010 Walden Ave., P.O. Box 1325, Buffalo, NY 14269
Canadian: P.O. Box 609, Fort Erie, Ont. L2A 5X3

DAPHNE CLAIR

Grounds for Marriage

Harlequin Books

TORONTO • NEW YORK • LONDON
AMSTERDAM • PARIS • SYDNEY • HAMBURG
STOCKHOLM • ATHENS • TOKYO • MILAN
MADRID • WARSAW • BUDAPEST • AUCKLAND

ISBN 0-373-11866-X

GROUNDS FOR MARRIAGE

First North American Publication 1997.

CHAPTER ONE

IT SHOULDN'T be difficult to tell him, Lacey thought, tipping a tray of warm, sweet-smelling biscuits onto the wire rack to cool.

Her ears, alert for the sound, identified the muted hum of the Peugeot's engine as the car swept into the drive outside, then the double slam of the doors, and Emma's childish voice answered by Tully's deep masculine one.

Lacey took a shaking breath. There was no reason for the flutter of nerves in her midriff, the unsteadiness of her hand as she picked up a biscuit that had dropped onto the counter and placed it on the rack. She stowed away the tray and pushed back a tress of light brown hair that had fallen across her cheek, curving it behind her ear with one finger.

Then the door burst open and Emma came in, her face flushed and eyes alight, wisps of dark, fine hair escaping from the hood of her padded windbreaker.

'Mum, we've been horse-riding—it was neat fun! The lady said I've got a natural seat. Can I please have a pony of my own? *Please*?'

Emma was tall for a ten-year-old, taking after her father. Not for the first time, as Tully followed the child inside, Lacey thought how alike they were, with their near-black hair and inky blue eyes. Even some of Emma's mannerisms resembled his. Of course, she would never have Tully's masculine assurance, the underlying awareness of being male and liking it that was implicit in every movement he made. He couldn't even stand still without radiating a subtle sexual challenge to every adult

5

woman in the vicinity. It wasn't deliberate, just part of his personality.

Over Emma's head his amused eyes met Lacey's. The heat of the stove had warmed the small, primrose-painted kitchen, and one long-fingered hand slid down the zip of his fleece-lined jacket as he closed the door to shut out the gusty wind. According to the radio news the ski fields at Tongariro were deep in snow, and in the South Island farmers were losing lambs. It never snowed in Auckland, which was close to New Zealand's sub-tropical north, but grey days like this could be chilly.

Lacey said, 'Owning a pony is a big responsibility, Emma. And expensive. We've nowhere to keep a horse.' The suburban section on which the modest two-bedroom bungalow stood wasn't even big enough for them to have a dog.

Some of the glow died from Emma's face. 'We could find somewhere. I'd look after it. I look after Ruffles.'

'A cat is a bit different from a horse,' Lacey pointed out.

'Why?' Emma's voice held both disappointment and a hint of impending argument.

Tully ambled over to the counter and picked up a biscuit. 'For one thing, it's bigger,' he said. 'But we'll talk about it when you've had a bit more practice, Em.' He bit into the biscuit. 'Mm. This is good.'

Distracted, Emma asked, 'Can I have one?'

'They're not ready,' Lacey objected, eyeing Tully with exasperation as he grinned down at her, totally unintimidated. 'They've only just come out of the oven.'

'That's when they taste best,' Tully said, and took another, tossing it to Emma. 'Catch!'

She did so, giggling and then shooting a half-guilty, half-triumphant look at Lacey as she stuffed the biscuit into her mouth.

Giving up, Lacey took some cups from the hooks under the cupboards. 'I suppose you want coffee?' she asked Tully.

His mouth full of biscuit, he nodded, moving aside to allow her to reach the coffee maker.

'Sit down,' she said. 'Emma, when you've finished that go and hang up your jacket, and then you can do your homework.'

'I'll do it afterwards,' Emma offered.

'Now. I told you if it wasn't done Friday night you'd have to do it Sunday afternoon.'

'I'll do it after tea.'

'You'll be tired.'

'But Daddy—'

'I want to talk to your father,' Lacey said firmly. 'Homework.'

Emma made a face and turned towards the door. Then she whirled, coming back to give Tully a hug. 'Thank you,' she said. 'I had the greatest time today!'

'Shut the door,' Lacey ordered as she left the room. Tully looked after her with a smile that faded as he turned towards Lacey. 'One biscuit won't hurt her,' he said.

Lacey poured coffee into two cups and set them on the laminated table. Tully had taken off his jacket and hooked it onto the back of a chair before sitting down. In well-worn jeans, with the cuffs of his cotton shirt pushed back and the collar open, he looked more like a manual worker of some sort than the managing director of a highly successful business.

He said, 'Am I in for a lecture?' With a mixture of impatience and mock-solemnity he added, 'I'm sorry if I undermined your discipline.'

It wasn't what she'd wanted to talk to him about, but she seized on the issue as a delaying tactic. 'You do spoil her.'

For an instant his handsome face wore an expression that reminded her of Emma's when she was being stubborn. 'I don't see it that way.'

Inwardly Lacey sighed. 'How do you see it?' she asked.

Shrugging, he picked up his cup and stared into it without drinking. 'I can't be with her every day like you,' he said, 'so I try to make up for it when we're together.'

'By letting her have everything she wants?' Lacey enquired dryly.

'By showing her that I care for her—as best I can.'

'Giving in to her every whim isn't necessarily the way to show it.'

He shot her an exasperated look. 'I don't do that. I've read some child psychology books, too. Emma's not a demanding child. What's the point of denying her a perfectly reasonable request when I can well afford it?'

'I'm not talking about the computer or the bicycle.' They'd had stiff little discussions about both when he had bought them.

'Right,' Tully said. 'Are we talking about one biscuit?'

Lacey shook her head. 'Of course not. It's just that you...'

She hadn't meant the conversation to go this way. She'd pictured a friendly cup of coffee over a plate of fresh-baked biscuits, a few minutes of casual talk, and then herself saying, 'By the way...'

She jumped up and turned to the counter, scooping half a dozen biscuits onto a plate that she put down on the table before resuming her seat.

'A peace offering?' Tully looked from her to the plate and back again. 'Or coals of fire?'

Reluctantly, she smiled. 'Neither. Help yourself.'

He took one of the biscuits and bit off half of it, sipped some coffee and said, 'I get a kick out of watching her enjoy things. You don't really think having fun is bad for her, do you?'

She said sharply, 'It's all very well for you to treat her as a combination of playmate and pet. Someone has to impose some discipline in her life.'

Tully put his cup down, his eyes going darker. '*Someone* being you?'

'There is no one else—is there?' Her resentful hazel eyes met his.

A faint frown drew his black brows together. 'You've always said you could manage alone...'

'I have—for ten years. But apparently you don't agree with the way I've raised Emma.'

He looked at her for a moment and said, 'She's a lovely kid and a credit to you. But do you mind if I put in my two cents worth now and then?'

He'd put more—much more—than two cents worth into making Emma's life, and Lacey's, easier than it might have been. 'No,' she muttered finally. 'Of course I don't mind.'

'You're touchy today. It isn't like you.' He inspected her face searchingly. 'Is something wrong?'

It was her cue. Somehow it no longer seemed the right time to break the news, but she tried to smile and look happy. She *was* happy! 'There's nothing wrong,' she said. 'Just the opposite, in fact. I...have something to tell you. Even Emma doesn't know yet, because I thought she might blurt it out to you, and I would rather you heard it from me...' She stopped to take a wavery breath.

Tully looked warily alert, his strong hand curled about his cup on the table. 'So what is it?'

She swallowed, and said, 'I'm planning to get married.'

For perhaps three seconds Tully didn't move, just sat staring at her, his expression a total blank.

Then he moved like an explosion, scraping his chair away from the table so it screeched on the floor and the jacket hanging over the back swung violently. '*You're what?*'

Looking at him looming over her, Lacey blinked. 'I'm getting married,' she repeated. 'You heard me.'

Tully shook his head as though to clear it. 'I heard. I just didn't believe it.'

'I don't see why not,' she said tartly. 'I'm free and way past twenty-one—but not exactly over the hill yet—sane, not suffering from any communicable disease, and have all my own teeth . . .'

'All right!' Tully cut in gratingly. 'I wasn't trying to be insulting.'

'Well, be sure to tell me when you *are* trying so I'll know the difference!'

He gave a reluctant crack of laughter. 'It was just . . . unexpected.' He hooked the chair round with his foot so that its back faced her, dropping down astride it with his chin resting on his folded arms along the back. His eyes looked black and brilliant, fixing intently on her. 'So . . .' he said. 'Who's the lucky man?'

Lacey relaxed slightly. The worst was over. 'His name's Julian,' she said. 'Julian Wye. He's a solicitor.'

'Emma's never mentioned any Julian Wye. How long have you known him?'

'I first met him a couple of years ago. He was a friend of a friend.'

'And now he's *your* friend. Your . . . fiancé?'

'It's not official yet. There are complications.'

'What sort of complications?'

'For one thing Emma may need time to get used to the idea, and Julian has a sixteen-year-old daughter—'

Tully's head lifted as he straightened. 'How old is this guy?'

'Thirty-nine. He's—'

'He's too old for you!'

'I don't think so. Anyway, it's not relevant.'

'You want to marry some guy who's nearly forty, and you think it's not relevant?'

'I'm nearly thirty.'

'No, you're not,' he argued. '*I'm* not even thirty yet. He's a dozen years older than you!'

'Eleven. Anyway,' she said, brushing aside the question of relative ages, 'the thing is, I need your help.'

'Whoa!' Tully said. 'Just hang on a minute. What about the mother of this sixteen-year-old daughter of his? Is he divorced?'

'She died,' Lacey said. 'Julian had to bring up Desma by himself.'

'And she lives with him?'

'Of course. He's her father.'

'I'm Emma's father.'

'That's different.'

'Is it? I thought there was only one way to father a child. Leaving aside test-tubes ...'

'You know what I mean.'

'Ah. You mean we weren't married.' He paused. 'You know the offer is still open.'

'No, thanks!' Lacey said decisively, and saw unexpected anger flare deep in his eyes. She supposed her vehemence had been less than tactful. 'We've discussed all that,' she reminded him.

'Not for a long time. Years, in fact.'

'Nothing's changed.'

'But apparently it has. Or it's about to. You can't tell me that everything will stay the same if you marry this ... Julian.'

She moistened her lower lip with her tongue. 'That's why I wanted to talk to you. I don't want Emma to feel she has to choose between you and him. I need you to help her understand that it's okay to grow fond of her new ... her stepfather.'

For a while she was afraid he wasn't going to answer, then he got up off the chair again and went to lean back against the counter, one foot hooked over the other ankle, his thumbs thrust into the waistband of his jeans. It was a casual attitude but he didn't look casual. He looked like a large, wary, wild animal debating whether or not to attack. 'I don't know,' he said. 'It's not as simple as that.'

A prickle of annoyance ran along her spine. 'It's for Emma's sake,' she said. 'Surely you can see that?' She assured him, 'It won't make any difference to your time with her. Julian knows that you have access to Emma, and he thoroughly approves.'

'Good of him.'

'I wouldn't have considered marrying him if he'd suggested you stop seeing Emma,' Lacey said quietly. 'You know I'd never do anything that might hurt her.'

'*You* won't. How do you know what he might do?'

'He's not that sort of person. And it will be good for Emma to have a man in the house.'

'I thought you were quite satisfied with our arrangement.'

'It was the best we could do for her, and of course she will still feel the same about you.' She hesitated, then said, 'Tully, you're not jealous, are you?'

'Jealous?' He cast her a strange, surprised look. His eyes were nearly opaque as they drifted from her face to the baggy T-shirt and faded jeans disguising a figure that had long since lost its teenage chubbiness but would never be really slim, although the generous swell of her breasts and hips made her waist look smaller than it actually was.

'Emma,' Lacey said hastily, 'loves you. Julian doesn't want to replace you in any way.'

'Oh yes, he does,' Tully murmured almost absently, his gaze still on what he could discern of her body, not her face. 'In at least one way he does.'

Made uncomfortable by his scrutiny, Lacey stood up and swept the coffee cups off the table to dump them in the sink. Turning on the hot tap, she said crossly, 'You know that's nonsense.'

Tully remained leaning on the counter beside her, his eyes thoughtful as he watched her rinsing the cups. 'Did you tell Emma not to mention Julian to me?'

'No, of course not!' She stepped back to take a tea-towel from the wall. 'Why would I do that?'

He shrugged. 'I just think it's a bit odd that she's never said anything. Seeing you and he are so...close.'

Lacey was vigorously drying a cup. 'Maybe she has talked about him but you didn't notice. She chatters a lot.'

A smile momentarily curved his mouth. 'She does. But if she'd mentioned anyone who's special to you I'd have noticed.'

Carefully, Lacey hung the cup on a hook and picked up the remaining one. 'She hasn't seen all that much of him. We've been meeting each other mostly when Emma's with you.'

'And you haven't told her that?'

'Not every time.' Why was she feeling so defensive? 'She isn't all that interested in what I do when she's away. Children are pretty self-centred.'

Once or twice Julian had offered to include Emma in an outing. She had politely declined a visit to the zoo, saying she'd seen it before and didn't think zoos were a good idea anyway. And although she'd enjoyed Kelly Tarlton's Underwater World on Auckland's waterfront, most of her knowledgeable comments on the sharks, fish and other denizens of the deep had been addressed to her mother. All Julian's remarks had been answered in monosyllables.

When Lacey had asked Julian to come to the house for a meal, hoping that he could get to know her daughter better, Emma had made it obvious without being in the least bad-mannered that staying around the grown-ups bored her, and had asked permission to go off and do her own thing.

After Julian left, Lacey had asked her casually, 'Do you like Julian, Emma?'

Emma, her eyes innocent and surprised, shrugged. 'He's all right, I s'pose, for a grown-up.'

'I think he's very nice,' Lacey said cautiously. 'He likes you very much.' He'd said she was a nice, well-behaved child.

'He's your friend,' Emma said with patent indifference, 'not mine. Can I have Riria over to play after school tomorrow?'

And that just about summed up their conversations about Julian, Lacey realised. Either Emma was oblivious to the fact that Julian was different from her mother's other friends, or she was deliberately shutting out the possibility. Lacey suspected the latter, which was why she needed Tully's help.

'I want you to reassure her,' she said, 'that it isn't going to cause any change to your relationship.'

'How can you know that?' Tully sounded slightly edgy, almost irritable.

Turning from hanging up the tea-towel, Lacey stared at him, perplexed, and with a hint of foreboding in the pit of her stomach. 'You wouldn't let it, surely!'

He stopped lounging against the counter and his hands gripped it behind him. 'I may not have the choice,' he said. 'You don't think you can just foist a stepfather on the child and expect it to make no difference, do you?'

'I'm not *foisting* Julian on Emma! I'm trying to go about this in the most sensitive way possible. That's exactly why I wanted to talk to you first! So that you could help her to make the adjustment.'

'You're taking a lot for granted.'

She said coldly, 'I thought I could take it for granted that you love Emma and want what's best for her.'

Tully shifted his position, folding his arms as he leaned back on the counter again. His eyelids drooped a little and his voice was clipped when he said, 'That's exactly why I want to know more about this prospective bride-groom of yours. How can I be sure he's a suitable step-father for my daughter?'

'I'd have thought you'd trust my judgement!'

His brows lifted in derision. 'Your judgement?' he queried, with the faintest emphasis.

'I might have been lacking in it when I was seventeen,' she said somewhat waspishly, 'but I've developed some discrimination since then.'

He gave a silent whistle, a gleam of appreciation in his eyes. 'You pack a punch when your dander's up, don't you?' He added thoughtfully, 'I can't recall that I've ever seen you in a real temper.'

'Don't push your luck.'

He laughed. 'I'm only thinking of Emma's welfare—and yours.'

'I can look after my own welfare, thank you. And Emma's. You know I wouldn't risk making her unhappy.'

'Not knowingly,' he conceded. 'But the soundest judgement can be clouded by love.'

'You'd know.' He had enough experience.

He laughed again, shortly. '*I'm* not in love with Julian. Maybe I should meet him.'

Strangely reluctant, she looked at him without answering, until his quizzical expression forced her to say something. 'Do you really feel that's necessary?'

'We're bound to bump into each other sooner or later,' he pointed out. 'If you want my co-operation, Lacey, I insist on meeting him. I won't hand my daughter over to another man without knowing what sort of guy he is.'

'You're not being asked to hand her over!'

'If he's going to be her stepfather,' Tully insisted, 'it amounts to something like it.'

He had a point, although it galled her that Tully wouldn't take her word for the fact that Julian was entirely trustworthy. 'He's brought up a daughter of his own,' she said.

'You said there was a problem there.'

'I said it's a complication,' Lacey protested. 'We don't know how the girls will get on.'

'They haven't met?'

'No.' She'd met Desma several times but couldn't claim to be close to her. From Julian she'd gathered that his daughter was in the difficult phase of mild rebellion common to many teenagers. 'We both realise that we need to take our time, let the girls get used to the idea.'

'Supposing they don't like each other?'

'We'll cross that bridge when—if—we come to it. Emma's not difficult to get along with.'

'Desma's older. What if she bullies Emma?'

'That's hardly likely,' Lacey argued. 'With the age gap, she'd more likely ignore a younger child altogether.'

Tully frowned. 'Desma's an only child?'

'Yes, she is.'

'Then she's accustomed to having her father to herself, I presume. If she's jealous she could take it out on Emma.'

'I'll be on the watch for it,' Lacey assured him with determined patience. 'And I'm sure Julian won't allow her to do that.'

'Desma's *his* daughter. What if he takes her side?'

'For heaven's sake, Tully! All these problems are purely theoretical.'

'You ought to be prepared for them,' Tully warned. 'They're common enough in blended families.'

'Maybe you should set yourself up as a counsellor,' she suggested, with more than a hint of sarcasm, 'as you're so knowledgeable about these things.'

'I'm not claiming any special knowledge. I've seen some of my friends in similar situations, and read a few articles. Common sense should tell you it's not going to be easy.'

'Do you think the last ten years have been easy for me?'

She saw him visibly stiffen, as though she'd accused him. 'I've done all I can to make it so,' he said.

'I know that.' She looked at him helplessly. 'You've done more than most men would have in the circumstances, and I'm grateful—'

He made an impatient gesture. 'I owed it to you...and to Emma.'

'I agree you owed it to Emma,' she said, 'but it would have been easy to walk away. That's what everyone fully expected you to do.'

His jaw tightened. 'You certainly have a great idea of my character.'

'You were nineteen. It would have been understandable. But maybe now you owe it to Emma to help me establish a more normal family life for her.'

'Are you saying you're doing this for Emma's sake?' Tully enquired.

At the deliberate mockery and conjecture in his gaze, she felt a slight heat on her cheeks. 'No, I'm not saying that. But it is a consideration.'

'Be honest, Lacey,' he said brutally. 'You've got the hots for this Julian, and you want me to make it easy for you by talking Emma round.'

Her hands went out to close on the back of the nearest chair. 'That's a foul thing to say! And it's not true!'

'I'm sorry if you find my language too basic. You're not going to pretend that sex doesn't enter into it?'

'Sex is a very small part of love. There are much more important things.'

'Really? Tell me about them.'

'Respect, for one. And consideration—tenderness, sharing...'

He made a disparaging little sound. 'Does Julian think sex is unimportant?'

'I didn't say it's unimportant.'

'A *small* part of love? That doesn't sound as though you place much importance on it.'

'One thing I learned from my experience with you,' she said acidly, 'is that sex on its own is worth nothing!'

An oddly bleak expression flickered across his face. Then he asked, 'Isn't Emma worth something?'

'I wouldn't be without her for anything in the world. You know that! But at the time the last thing on our minds was making a baby.' A starkly vivid memory flash caught her unawares, and her pulse rate momentarily increased.

'That doesn't mean it was worthless. At the time it meant a great deal to me. You were sweet and caring, and I felt very...grateful.'

'You were drunk,' Lacey reminded him ruthlessly. 'And maudlin. The thing is, Emma does exist, and I'm trying to do the best for her. But I...I have needs, too.'

'Needs?' He scanned her face, and her skin burned.

'I'd like a real family,' she said steadily. 'I want to be married.'

'I've offered you marriage. More than once.'

She gave a tiny shrug, her lips tugging into a smile. 'And I appreciate the offer, Tully, but it wouldn't work.'

'How do you know it wouldn't work? We get on all right.'

They did, when he came to collect Emma, or just dropped in and ended up staying for a meal. And on the fairly rare occasions that he'd persuaded Lacey to join them for an outing. But he'd never really wanted to marry her. He'd be doing it for Emma. 'We get on fine,' she agreed, 'as far as we need to for Emma's sake. It's quite different from sharing a home and...'

'And a bed,' he finished for her.

It wasn't what she'd been going to say, but she let that go.

'All right,' he said abruptly. 'I won't promise anything, but I'll keep an open mind. Only I'm not going to try to influence Emma, not until I meet this guy.'

Lacey supposed she could hardly ask more. She'd always been glad that Tully had been so ready to acknowledge Emma as his child and spend so much time with her. This was just a manifestation of his love and concern, so she shouldn't complain. 'I'll try to arrange something.'

'Yes, do that.' He reached over and retrieved his jacket, swinging it across his shoulder. Again she saw a speculative, slightly surprised and perhaps even calculating gleam in his dark eyes as he stood for a moment or two just looking at her.

He was probably wondering what Julian saw in her. But not every man was spoiled for choice. 'I'll call Emma,' she said hastily, 'and tell her you're leaving.'

As usual they walked out to the car with him. Emma returned his hug and kiss with gusto, and then he turned to Lacey. Expecting the customary peck on her cheek, she stood with her hand on Emma's shoulder and lifted her face.

But this time, instead of brushing her cheek his lips came down warmly against hers, pressing them apart.

Lacey stepped back, her eyes flying wide, to find him looking at her with a mixture of challenge and curiosity. Then he abruptly turned and got into the driver's seat, slamming the door and giving Emma a wave and a smile before backing out.

Confused, Lacey stared after the receding car. Her heart was pounding and she could still feel the possessive imprint of his kiss on her mouth.

What on earth had he meant by it?

CHAPTER TWO

'OF COURSE I'll meet Emma's father,' Julian said. 'She's a lucky little girl that he's so concerned about her welfare.'

They were sitting in his car on Lacey's driveway at the conclusion of a rare evening date, Emma having been invited to stay overnight at a friend's house. It had been a treat for Lacey to see a show and share a leisurely supper without having to worry about getting home to let a baby-sitter off the hook. Most of her outings were daytime ones, when Emma was at school or out with Tully, and when she ate out it was generally lunch with a friend.

Julian had chosen a North Shore restaurant, driving over the Harbour Bridge at dusk while the light of the dying sun still sheened the waters of the Waitemata. After leaving the restaurant he had switched on the car heater against the wintry coolness of the night, making Lacey feel warm and pampered, replete with adult conversation and delicious food. And he had responded in his customary amiable, reasonable manner to her relaying of Tully's request.

'You're such a nice man!' she told him gratefully.

He chuckled, drawing her closer and rubbing his cheek gently against her temple. 'Thank you. I'm very glad you think so. I hope your daughter will come to the same conclusion. I want to get to know her properly.' His mouth touched her cheek, and wandered, seeking her lips.

20

Lacey returned his kiss, and let him push open her jacket and stroke her body, liking the pleasurable, tingling feelings he aroused.

After a few minutes Julian drew back, breathing heavily. 'I'm too old for necking in a car,' he said humorously. 'Are you going to invite me in, Lacey?'

He must have noticed her hesitation, and she felt him begin to move away.

'Yes,' she said, 'if you like. But—'

'I'm not trying to rush you into bed,' he assured her. 'I absolutely respect your views. When you have a daughter it's important to live by the values you try to impart to her.'

'I'll make coffee,' she offered, groping for the door handle.

When he left half an hour later, she washed up the coffee cups and told herself that her feeling of flatness and dissatisfaction was caused by physical frustration.

She'd been repressing her sexuality for years, quite deliberately and not without difficulty. If occasionally a stirring of desire had made itself felt she had ruthlessly quelled it. She had a child who was her first priority, and a close relationship with a man would only cause unnecessary complications in her life. She'd concentrated on keeping herself too busy to be bothered. Apart from looking after Emma, she had taken courses in computer keyboarding and office procedures so that she could work from home, and then embarked on a part-time degree course in business administration which she'd now nearly completed.

Tully had been intrigued by her choice and her determination, and she'd been grateful for his help, freely offered from his own experience of both university study and running his own business. The one thing she wouldn't do was work for his firm, feeling that it smacked too much of either charity or a form of nepotism.

Tully was the only man she had room for in her life, and that was strictly on a platonic basis. Anything else would be courting disaster and heartbreak. For Emma's sake as well as her own, she wouldn't risk that.

She had occasionally been the recipient of advances from other men. Some rather obviously felt they were doing her a favour, and had been astonished when she rebuffed them. But on first meeting Julian she was totally unaware of any sexual overtones. She'd found him easy to talk to, friendly and sincere, and they'd had something in common, both being solo parents.

Despite his successful legal practice his manner was rather diffident, and she'd been surprised when she learned his age, because his smooth, pleasant face and the fine, straight brown hair combed back from a high forehead, combined with the slightness of his tall frame, gave him a youthful air.

She'd known him casually for almost a year before he asked her out, and he had courted her with gentleness and sensitivity, always ready to back off if she was hesitant about going too fast.

Like tonight, she thought as she pulled a shapeless brushed-cotton nightgown over her head. He hadn't even touched her after they'd got inside, unless she counted the quick hug and kiss he'd given her before he left. He'd sat at the table with a finger threaded through the handle of his cup as he drank his coffee, and talked companionably about the show they'd seen, about the latest headline news, and for quite a long time about his daughter who, to his considerable concern, had acquired a boyfriend whom Julian suspected of having a delinquent past.

She had found herself picturing Tully sitting across from her instead, remembering the way he always curled his entire hand about his cup and firmly held it. And then for some reason she'd remembered the sure, compelling pressure of his lips on hers, not at all like Julian's tender, carefully inquiring kisses.

She'd felt a sudden irritation as Julian went on worrying aloud about Desma. Brushing it aside, she chided herself for selfishness and tried to concentrate and make helpful comments. She knew how anxiety about a much-loved child could oust everything else from a parent's mind.

Just before he left she'd suppressed an impulse to suggest they move to the sofa in the living room. Her need to be held, to feel close to someone for a while, for the comfort of a masculine shoulder to lean on temporarily, might be interpreted as an invitation to go further than she intended. And it would hardly be fair to Julian to raise expectations she didn't mean to fulfil.

Climbing into bed, Lacey sighed. She would fulfil those expectations eventually, of course. She'd promised to marry Julian—when their respective daughters had accepted the idea. Sex with Julian would be . . . nice. She was sure of it.

Lacey had suggested that Julian come round for an evening meal the next time Tully had Emma for the day. That way, she thought, Emma would see that Tully didn't object to her mother having a male friend, and the men would have a chance to get to know each other after Emma had gone to bed.

Julian arrived quite early. When Tully and Emma came in he was sitting at the kitchen table. Dressed in grey slacks and a soft yellow pullover over a spotless paler yellow shirt, he'd been drinking white wine while Lacey stirred a sauce on the stove.

Pushing her hair back from a face warmed by the heat of the stove, Lacey removed the sauce from the glowing ring and introduced the two men. 'Julian, this is Tully Cleaver.'

Julian got to his feet and extended his hand. 'I'm very pleased to meet Emma's father,' he said.

Tully, ripping open the zip of his jacket, subjected the other man to a piercing appraisal, then nodded and briefly shook hands. His dark hair had tiny rain-beads on it and he carried the clean, fresh scent of the outdoors with him.

The cat, a large, fluffy black animal with a white ruff, bib and paws, had followed Emma inside. She scooped it up into her arms, and Tully reached over and absently scratched behind the velvety black ears, his eyes hardly moving from Julian, who had resumed his seat at the table. The cat set up a loud, rattling purr.

'You can feed Ruffles now, Emma, before you take off your jacket,' Lacey suggested. 'Tully, can I get you a drink?'

'I'll do it,' he said easily, casting a glance at Julian's half-empty glass. 'Can I pour some more for you?' he asked. 'What have you got?'

'Dry white, thank you.'

'It's in the fridge,' Lacey told him. 'I'll have one, too.' She opened the oven for a quick check on the roast.

Tully hung his coat over a chair and took a wineglass from the cupboard. He filled it from the chilled bottle in the refrigerator and handed it to Lacey, then topped up Julian's glass and poured himself a whisky from the supply that Lacey kept for him.

'Why don't we go into the other room?' Lacey said. The kitchen seemed overcrowded now, although Emma had taken the cat food and a spoon and gone outside to feed Ruffles.

In the living room she had lit a fire. Julian went to one of the chairs set at right angles to the fireplace, and Tully stood near the other as Lacey sank down on the sofa. But when Julian had taken his seat, to Lacey's surprise Tully moved and came to share the sofa with her, lounging in the corner with his arm lying along the back.

She looked down into her wineglass, and heard Tully say to Julian, 'Lacey tells me you're a solicitor. That means you don't do court work, doesn't it?'

'It's not my field, no.' Julian's light, precise voice was pleasant and even. 'I do quite a lot of conveyancing. Property transfers, you know.'

'Yes,' Tully said. 'I do know.'

'Lacey hasn't told me what you do.'

Hearing the faint questioning note in his voice, Lacey looked up and saw the way Julian's eyes passed rapidly over Tully's casual shirt and well-used jeans.

Tully took a swig from his glass. 'I make marine safety equipment,' he said. 'At least, the firm does.'

'What firm is that?'

'Cleaver's,' Tully said shortly.

'A family business?'

After a moment Tully said, 'That's right.' It had been a family business, founded by Tully's grandfather, but Lacey knew that Tully now owned the New Zealand branch, having bought out his father who lived and operated his factories in Australia.

'I think I read something about it recently,' Julian mused. 'You're branching out from life-jackets and emergency craft into manufacturing some new type of rubber-and-wool boom to contain oil spills?'

'And mop them up. Yes.'

'It sounds very worthwhile, a real contribution towards preserving the environment.'

Tully swirled the whisky in his glass. 'It's also going to make the firm a good bit of money, I hope.'

Julian smiled uncertainly. 'I'm sure there's nothing wrong in that.' He took a quick sip from his wineglass.

Lacey tried to think of something with which to fill the ensuing silence. 'Have you and Emma been riding again?' she asked Tully.

He smiled, turning his head to look into her eyes. 'Try to keep her away. It's true what she said. She does seem to be a natural on a horse.'

'You're an experienced rider?' Julian looked interested.

Tully almost reluctantly dragged his eyes from Lacey. 'I'm learning along with Emma,' he said. 'I was quoting the instructor.'

Julian's brows rose in surprise. 'That's very commendable. Sharing Emma's interests—I take off my hat to you, Tully.'

'Thanks,' Tully drawled, eyeing Julian with a look of judicious speculation. 'Actually, I'm enjoying it.'

Emma came into the room, and Tully smiled at her, immediately shifting over to make room on the end of the sofa. His hip pressed against Lacey's, his arm sliding further along behind her. If she leaned back a little she knew he would lay it casually about her shoulders. She didn't lean back.

Julian smiled at Emma. 'Your father's been telling us about your riding lessons, Emma. Have you fallen off, yet?'

'I don't fall off,' she told him loftily. 'If you use your hands and your knees the right way you won't fall.'

Lacey wrenched her attention away from Tully. 'I don't know, I have a feeling I might fall off all the same.'

'No, you wouldn't,' Emma said with great confidence. 'I'd stop you—or Daddy. Wouldn't we?' she appealed to her father.

He grinned down at her. 'We'd certainly do our best. But don't forget, you and I are just learners, and they do say pride goes before a fall.' Turning back to Lacey, he said, 'Maybe you should join us next time. We could all give it a go.'

He was very close. She could smell the warm scent of his body, still carrying a faint tang of the outdoors. Her eyes were drawn to the outline of his mouth, the faintly

shadowed male perfection of his skin. At this distance—
or lack of it—his blatant masculinity was overwhelming.

'Maybe,' she said, deliberately shifting her gaze
beyond him to Julian. 'Should we, Julian? Do you think
you'd enjoy riding?'

'I think my riding days are over,' he said. 'I gave it
up a long time ago.'

'You used to ride? I didn't know that.'

'When I was a boy,' he said, adding rather modestly,
'I collected a few ribbons at shows.'

Oh, joy! She felt Tully sit up straighter beside her as
his eyes swivelled to Julian. Emma had turned too,
staring at Julian with new respect.

'What sort of ribbons?' Emma asked him.

'Dressage and show-jumping.'

'What's dressage?' Emma asked.

As Julian began to explain, Lacey went to check the
dinner. She needed to remove herself from Tully. He
ought to carry a health label—Warning: Proximity May
Endanger Your Heart. Though surely hers was safe.
She'd given it to Julian. And she'd had plenty of practice
at ignoring her natural female response to Tully's blatant
masculinity.

She set a bowl of pansies in the centre of the dining
table. They seldom used this room for its avowed
purpose—usually it served as an office for Lacey's typing
and desk-top publishing business. Her word-processor,
printer and photocopier occupied a long bench spanning
one wall, while filing cabinets sat underneath, and the
extendible dining table was useful for collating pages or
making up layouts.

'Mum, shall I set the table?' Emma stood in the
doorway.

Surprised, Lacey turned. 'If you'd like to. I thought
you'd be talking to Julian about horses.'

Emma's face screwed up briefly. 'Mm. Daddy said to
come and ask if you needed any help.'

'Did he?' Lacey said grimly.

'What's the matter?'

'Nothing.' She smiled at Emma, banishing the suspicion that Tully had thought Julian was getting on too well with the child. Tully wasn't a mean-minded man. More likely he wanted to talk to Julian himself.

But she had to fight an impulse to rush back into the living room and monitor what the men were saying. 'Okay,' she told Emma. 'You set the table nicely while I turn over the potatoes.'

The meal went without any hitch, and the two men seemed cordial, if a bit formal with each other. Emma helped by chattering as usual, mostly to Tully. But when Julian put in a smiling question or remark here and there she answered politely enough.

'Bedtime,' Lacey told her after the dishes were cleared away and she'd been allowed to sit with them while they had coffee in the other room. 'Go and have your bath and put on your pyjamas, then you can come and say goodnight.'

When she did so, looking innocent and soapy-clean, she inveigled Tully into tucking her in, and he went off with a good grace, holding her hand.

'She has him wound around her little finger, doesn't she?' Julian remarked. He was sitting on an easy chair, and after dinner Lacey had chosen the one opposite, leaving the sofa for Tully and Emma.

'She adores him.' The fire was growing sluggish, and Lacey got up to put some wood on from the basket at the side of the hearth. Julian came over, removing the mesh fire screen, and replacing it for her as she straightened.

'It's going to be difficult,' he said, 'to compete.'

'You don't have to compete.' Lacey looked at him, her eyes troubled. 'It's a different relationship. I want her to be clear about that.'

'Mm. And do you think that when—if—I have to correct her, Emma will accept it from me? She's never had a real father, has she?' As Lacey opened her mouth to demur, he added, 'Tully's a weekend father, a fun-father, obviously. You told me he spoils her.'

She had said something of the sort once, when they were exchanging mutual confidences about their children and their problems. 'He does like to give her things, but she's not a spoiled child, is she?'

'She's a charmer,' Julian said dryly. 'And accustomed to being the centre of attention. I just wonder how she reacts when she isn't, or if she doesn't get her own way.'

Lacey felt a stirring of resentment, and reminded herself not to be oversensitive. 'Well, of course she sulks sometimes, or slams a few doors. She's only ten! But I don't give in to her, and I won't expect you to, either.'

He smiled. 'Well, that's all right then. As long as we back each other up there won't be too many problems.'

She made to return to her chair, but he caught her hands in his. 'It isn't a heavy criticism,' he said, giving her a wry, quizzical look. 'No child is perfect—heaven knows, Desma isn't! I expect you'll find I have my blind spots, too. You're not annoyed with me, are you?'

'No, of course not.' She smiled at him. It was a trifling point and he'd probably been right. She just wasn't used to anyone pointing out her daughter's small faults. Tully had certainly never done so, and he had every right, if anyone did...

Julian smiled back at her, obviously relieved. 'Good.' He leaned over and kissed her, his mouth moving persuasively on hers, coaxing a response.

'Sorry.' Tully's curt apology made Lacey start away from Julian in confusion, pulling her hands from his grasp.

Tully stood in the doorway with a thumb hooked into his belt, his expression sardonic. As he strolled into the room, Lacey took a step backwards and Julian ran a hand over his hair, turning away to look at the fire.

'Is Emma settled?' Lacey asked, resuming her chair and sitting very straight. She felt flustered, as though caught in a guilty act, and that was ridiculous.

'She's fine.' Tully dropped onto the sofa. Watching Julian sit down again, he asked, 'Where's your daughter tonight?'

'Seeing a film with some friends. I have to pick her up later.'

Tully nodded. 'She'll be off your hands soon, I suppose. How do you feel about being saddled with a pre-teen at this stage of your life?'

Julian seemed slightly startled, then made an effort at a smile. 'It doesn't bother me. I've had some practice. And I hope Desma will stick around for a few more years. Young people are staying home longer these days.' Relaxing a trifle, he added, 'I like children. My wife and I had hoped to have a couple more. Maybe...' He glanced across at Lacey, his eyes warm.

Tully shifted on the sofa, planting his feet more firmly apart on the carpet. 'You want another family,' he asked, 'at your age?'

Julian looked nettled, then amused. 'I'm not in my dotage.'

'Of course not,' Tully said after a telling moment. 'Prime of life, I'm sure.' His eyes were unfocused, but they sharpened as he turned to look at Lacey. 'Has your biological clock started ticking more loudly already?' he asked her. 'Do you want more kids?'

Swallowing anger, she said, 'That's something for Julian and me to discuss. I don't think it has anything to do with you.'

'If you're planning to produce a pack of half brothers and sisters for Emma, I think it does have something to do with me,' he said. 'It'll directly affect *her*. Isn't that the whole idea of this cosy after-dinner chat? If you want me to endorse this marriage of yours, I want to know just what sort of family life you're going to give my daughter.'

'We don't *need* your endorsement!' Lacey said. 'I just hoped it would make things easier all round.'

Julian cut in smoothly. 'There are still things that Lacey and I need to talk through. We're not in any great hurry.'

'You're not?' Tully looked at him with polite surprise. Then, his eyes narrowing, he turned his gaze to Lacey. 'I guess *you* have plenty of time.'

Julian cleared his throat. 'Tully,' he said, leaning forward to face the other man, 'I would like you to know that I admire and respect your willingness to take responsibility for...er...your youthful mistake. There aren't many men of your age who would have done what you have. Of course, by law you're obliged to financially support the child, but plenty of young fellows manage to wriggle out of that, and you've certainly gone much further than the letter of the law. All credit to you.'

Tully looked back at him woodenly. 'I appreciate the testimonial,' he said. 'Just where do you think all this flattery is going to get you?'

'Tully!' Lacey protested, but Julian held up a staying hand to her, giving a little laugh. 'It's all right, Lacey. Tully and I understand each other.'

Tully's dark brows lifted.

'The thing is,' Julian went on, 'the fact that Lacey chose to involve you at all in this is a matter of courtesy only. She actually isn't obliged to consult your wishes.' As Tully sat rigid and silent, he added, 'I'm sure you appreciate that.'

Lacey held her breath. Don't challenge Tully head-on, she wanted to warn Julian. He'll take on anybody and anything...and win.

For perhaps two seconds there was no movement, no sound in the room. Then Tully stood up, quite slowly, and rocked on his heels, both hands on his belt. 'Thanks for the free legal opinion,' he said, his voice quite pleasant. 'It's good to have the position clarified.'

Julian sat back, looking up at him rather cautiously. 'It's best we all know where we stand, don't you think?'

'Oh, undoubtedly.' Tully's reply was too quick, and far too cordial. Lacey saw the deep glint in his eyes and stiffened in her chair, but all he said was, 'I think I can do with another whisky, if you don't mind, Lacey. No, don't get up, I'll fetch it.' He turned to Julian. 'Care to join me? Or can I get you some more white wine?'

After the briefest hesitation Julian said, 'Thanks, I'll join you with a whisky.'

'Lacey?'

Lacey shook her head. 'Not for me.' This evening was definitely not going according to plan—the underlying friction was almost palpable. She could have done with a stiff drink, but a long time ago she'd had the value of a clear head in risky circumstances firmly implanted in her mind.

When Tully returned it was as though he'd decided to be as pleasant as possible for the remainder of the evening. He brought the whisky bottle with him, but after one glass Julian declined any more. 'I have to drive home and pick up Desma on the way,' he reminded them. 'I can't risk being over the limit.'

Tully poured himself another and nursed it while he questioned Julian about property values and the market forces, asked his opinion on a bill currently being debated in parliament designed to help lower-income home owners pay their mortgages, and listened with apparent attention to Julian's exposition of the relative merits of fixed rate and variable loans.

He seemed content to let Julian take over the conversation, merely injecting an occasional remark or query—some of them, Lacey felt, oddly naïve. By the time Julian moved on to explaining the impact of inflation on the building business, Lacey had to clench her jaws to hide an urge to yawn. She glanced at the electric clock on the wall, and saw Julian look at his watch.

With an exclamation of surprise, he stood up. 'I have to go, I'm afraid. Can't leave a teenager hanging about waiting at this hour. It's been nice meeting you, Tully.' He held out his hand and after a moment Tully rose and took it in his. 'I hope you feel confident now that Emma will be in good hands. And I'm sure Lacey's told you I have no objection at all to your continuing to see her as often as you like.'

Lacey waited for Tully to say he was leaving, too. When he didn't she saw Julian to the door, and exchanged a hurried, unsatisfactory kiss with him before he drove off. Tully, she saw, had parked his Peugeot on the road.

When she returned to the living room Tully was sitting hunched forward with his head bent, his forearms resting on his knees. The glass in his hand was still half full of whisky.

She paused in the doorway, and without turning round he said, 'Don't just stand there. Come and sit down.'

She walked past the sofa, but as she made for one of the chairs again he reached out and fastened a hand on her wrist. 'Not there.' He pulled her down beside him. 'I can't talk to you when you're halfway across the room.'

'It's only a few feet.' She tugged her hand from his grasp, but stayed on the sofa.

Tully gave her a crooked little smile. 'Don't argue, woman. It's friendlier this way.' He leaned back into the corner of the sofa, his eyelids drooping as he regarded her. Now that he had her where he wanted her, he didn't seem in a hurry to initiate conversation, so she decided to get in first.

'Why did you send Emma into the kitchen, earlier?' she asked him.

'To help you.'

'Not to get her away from Julian?' she challenged him. His eyelids flickered. 'How did you guess?'

'You admit it?' She was dismayed to have her suspicion so readily confirmed. If he was going to be deliberately unhelpful ...

'She was showing signs of terminal boredom. I didn't think you'd want her yawning in his face.'

'They were talking about horses! Which, thanks to you, she's crazy about at the moment.'

'Julian was talking, blinding the poor kid with science. She was way out of her depth.' He made a small grimace and shrugged. 'I guess he's not used to dealing with a ten-year-old any more.'

Lacey supposed that was so. He had certainly had difficulty hitting the right note with Emma over the dinner table. 'They need to get to know each other properly,' she said hopefully. 'Maybe Julian was trying a bit too hard tonight. He's very anxious for her to like him.'

Tully shifted his shoulders against the sofa back and stretched out his legs, contemplating the toes of his shoes for a second or two before shooting a hard, dark glance her way. 'Are you really in love with that guy?'

The faintly disbelieving note of near-contempt in his voice made her defensive. 'Of course I love Julian. He's a very nice person.' She moved uneasily, trying to relax. Somehow it wasn't his niceness that had shown up tonight. And in an obscure way she knew Tully was entirely responsible for that. 'I don't know what you were trying to do, but it won't work, Tully.'

'Trying to do?' he asked innocently. 'I thought I was being the almost perfect ... guest.'

She noticed the hesitation. Technically he might be a guest, but his place in her daughter's life made him more than that. Tonight he'd acted rather like a host trying his best to put a not-very-welcome guest at ease, and perhaps it was unfair of her to suspect any deliberation on his part. But she couldn't help feeling that he had set out to demonstrate his familiarity with the house and its occupants, to make Julian feel like an outsider. He'd even acted with a subtle possessiveness towards Lacey herself.

As if he'd been following her thoughts, Tully asked, 'Is where you're going to live one of the things you and Julian haven't discussed yet?'

'We're thinking about it. Julian's house has three bedrooms, so the girls wouldn't have to share a room. Or we could buy a new place.'

'So what will you do with this?'

'That's up to you.'

'It's half yours.'

Lacey shook her head. 'That was only a legal safeguard for Emma's sake, in case something happened to you. You paid for it.'

He didn't look pleased, but he apparently decided not to pursue the subject. Instead he stared broodingly at the dying fire, sipping at the whisky in his glass.

Lacey said quietly, 'Things change. Emma will get used to new surroundings, new circumstances. So will you.'

He turned to look at her, his eyes sombre. 'It won't be the same...will it?'

'No, it won't be the same.' She felt a twinge of sadness, a painful tug of regret, and deliberately hardened her heart. 'But it needn't affect your relationship with Emma.'

His mouth twisted in a strange sort of smile. 'As a matter of fact, I wasn't thinking of Emma. I was thinking of my relationship with you.'

'With...me?'

'We do have one, you know.'

'Of course,' she agreed. 'As Emma's parents...'

'Is that the only way you see me? As Emma's father?'

Lacey frowned uncertainly. What did he want her to say? Not for anything would she betray to him how difficult it had been to make herself think of him in that role alone, how long it had taken her to forsake foolish teenage dreams. If he wanted his ego stroked, there were plenty of other women who would do it for him—along with anything else he asked of them. 'How else should I see you?' she asked reasonably. 'If it wasn't for Emma we wouldn't have a relationship at all.'

He looked at her with speculation, as if considering the question. 'How can you be sure?' With spurious humility, he added, 'Hard to believe though it may be, most of the women I know don't actually view me first and foremost as a father.'

She didn't find it hard to believe at all. He had lost none of the male charisma he'd had at nineteen. If anything it had intensified with maturity, and in her case familiarity had not bred contempt, but rather a guarded awareness. Caught once in the trap of his careless sexuality, she had made up her mind a long time ago that she wasn't going to walk into it again. 'I'm sure they don't,' she said crisply. 'Fortunately, I know you better than most women do.'

His head cocked to one side, he said, 'I suppose you do.' He paused. 'Why "fortunately"?'

She'd hoped he wouldn't pick up on that. 'For one thing,' she said hastily, 'you don't have to worry that I'll try to drag you to the altar.'

His eyes were enigmatic, but very intent. 'Until recently I thought you had a distinct aversion to the state of matrimony yourself.'

'I never said that.'

'Mm. I gather that the aversion was to me.'

'Not to you personally. To the idea of marriage with you.'

'There's a difference?'

'Of course there's a difference. Marrying just to give Emma two parents would have been disastrous.'

'I agree it probably would have been when we were both teenagers. Although...' He shrugged. 'Who knows? It might have worked out okay.'

Lacey shook her head. 'We were too young.'

'Too young to be parents? I guess so—objectively. But Emma's okay.'

'Yes. At least we got that right.'

'*You* did. I'm well aware that I'm only a part-time father. And now...' she was surprised at the fierce regret she saw in his face '...someone else may get the chance that I never had.'

'I'm sorry,' she said awkwardly. 'I didn't know you felt so strongly about it.'

'Didn't you?' His glance was almost hostile, before he got up and went to stand looking at the remains of the fire, his hand resting on the mantel above it. 'No,' he said. 'How could you? I hardly knew myself.' He turned to look at her searchingly. 'You're entitled to look for a bit of happiness. Heaven knows I've no right stop you. But are you sure it's Julian you want?'

'I'm old enough now to know exactly what I want,' she said unequivocally, pushing away a small, nagging doubt. Of course she and Julian had a tacit understanding that much depended on their children's reactions, but neither of them had expected any major problems to arise.

Why, just when Tully seemed to be capitulating completely to the idea, did she suddenly feel afraid, unsure of herself and of the future to which she'd virtually committed both herself and Emma? Saying it aloud in an unconscious effort to dispel the fear, she declared, 'Julian and I love each other. I've told him I'll marry him, and that's what I intend to do.'

He looked at her silently, apparently weighing her answer.

Moving restlessly under his probing gaze, Lacey said, 'So can I count on you letting Emma know that it's all right with you?'

'Don't rush me,' he said softly, and although his eyes remained on her face she had the impression that his mind had gone off on a tangent. 'I'm thinking about it.'

'How long do you need to think?'

He came away from the mantel. 'I'll let you know. Julian said there's no hurry...'

That last almost sounded like a question, but she didn't comment.

Stopping in front of her, he put a hand lightly under her chin, stooping towards her.

Remembering the last time he'd kissed her goodbye, Lacey instinctively turned her face aside.

His fingers tightened, forcing her to look at him. He was close; she could see the fine lines at the corners of his eyes, and as she watched his pupils dilated, filled with dark fire. She saw her own uplifted face reflected in them, felt an answering lick of fire deep inside her, an unwilled hunger.

Then Tully released her and stepped back. His chest moved with a quick breath. Somehow he looked nearly as disconcerted as Lacey felt.

She stood up. 'I'll see you out.'

'Don't bother.'

He gave her another probing, appraising look and left her staring rather blankly after him as he strode out of the room. A minute later she heard the outer door close.

CHAPTER THREE

WHEN Tully telephoned her a few days later Lacey's first hope was that he'd thought over her suggestion and decided to agree.

But instead he said, 'I've been inveigled into taking part in a charity "Welcome to Spring" water derby at Mission Bay on Sunday. I thought Emma might like to come along and watch her old man get a dunking or two.'

'I'm sure she'd love it. I'll ask her for you.'

'You'd have to come, too. I don't want to leave her on her own, especially near water. She could bring along a friend if she wants to, but they'd need an adult nearby.'

'No convenient girlfriend at the moment?' Lacey inquired rather dryly.

'No current girlfriend,' he confirmed. 'So, are you free?'

On Saturday she and Julian had planned to introduce their daughters to each other over a Chinese brunch at a restaurant in the city and take them to a film. But Sunday they'd decided to spend apart. 'I can come,' she said. 'What time shall we be there?'

'There could be parking problems, but I've got a competitor's pass. I'll pick you up about ten.'

Emma had invited her friend Riria along, and they sat in the back seat of the car chattering while Lacey asked Tully, 'How, exactly, did you get inveigled into this?'

'I'm a ring-in. Some of the guys in the firm have been practising for weeks—we've been sponsoring their entry—but one of them came down with some kind of bug yesterday. It was going to be difficult finding a replacement at short notice, so I got volunteered for the job.'

'It's a team effort?'

'There are some individual events but I'm part of a team, yes. We rack up points for every event entered, then the big one is the raft race at the end. Apparently anything goes, short of drowning the opposition.'

'Sounds like fun,' Lacey said.

'It sounds highly uncomfortable. And I expect you and Emma to give due appreciation to my efforts for the cause.'

'What do we do? Sponsor you? Lay bets on you?'

'There'll be people going round with buckets for donations. But I meant you can cheer me on . . . and cheer me up if we lose.'

'What if you win?'

'Ah! Then I expect the usual winner's perks.'

'I didn't know I was supposed to bring a laurel wreath.'

He glanced at her. 'It wasn't a laurel wreath I was thinking of.' His gaze slipped to her mouth briefly before he returned his attention to the road.

About to snap at him, *I'm not one of your girlfriends!* she stopped herself. He hadn't said anything, really. And even if he had meant what she thought—which he had—it was only banter. That kind of thing came naturally to him; she'd been deflecting it for years without particularly thinking about it.

The day turned out to be a lot of fun, at least for the enthusiastic onlookers gathered on the grassy reserve along the beach front, and watching from balconies and vantage points among the houses and commercial buildings a road's width from the beach. The Waitemata was dotted with small sailing craft dipping and twirling between the bay and the gentle distant slopes of Rangitoto, the island volcano that dominated the harbour.

Officially it was the first day of spring, and balmy sunshine promised a real New Zealand summer, but the water temperature was still wintry.

There were novelty swimming races for the hardy— or foolhardy—involving balloons, inflatable toys and various other props. Dressed in a wetsuit, Tully took part in a couple of those with his team, and they came second in a round-the-buoy relay. Emma was ecstatic when he returned to them after he had changed back into jeans and a woollen shirt, his damp hair slick and black.

To vary the programme a team of life-savers gave a demonstration, and there was a race between three long Maori canoes, their crews sporting the swirling blue patterns of traditional tattoos on their faces, most of them applied with ink but a few the genuine article. The event was one of the most thrilling of the day, the paddles flashing in and out of the water in an increasingly fast rhythm. Afterwards the winners performed a rousing victory haka on the beach, delighting the spectators.

Emma declared she was hungry, and Tully handed her some money and sent her off with Riria to the mobile stands selling hot dogs, chips, waffles and doughnuts.

He and Lacey stood watching the two girls thread their way through the crowd. A gust of wind blew Lacey's hair across her eyes and she pushed it back, the movement catching Tully's attention. He looked down at her and smiled. 'Sometimes you look so much like Emma—or she like you.'

'She's like *you*!' Lacey said, startled.

'Her colouring, yes. But in the shape of her face she takes after you, and her hair's fine and soft like yours...' Idly he reached out a hand, lifting the strands and letting them fall against her cheek. Then, before she could do it, he carefully hooked them behind her ear, his fingers brushing her cheek, lingering a little before he let his hand fall.

Lacey found it difficult to wrench her gaze away from his, and instinctively she took a half step back.

It's nothing, she assured herself as she deliberately searched for and found Emma's bright jacket. Tully was an attractive man, she'd always known that. It wasn't the first time over the years that she had become momentarily—*momentarily*, she assured herself—acutely conscious of it. Few women would have been totally unmoved by him. Yet he'd probably be astonished if she told him that his casual gesture had made her blood race.

When the girls came back with the food Tully found a sheltered spot on the grass for them to sit on. Perhaps it was the presence of her friend, Lacey thought, but Emma was clearly having a much more enjoyable time than she'd had the day before, when Julian had taken them and Desma out.

The girls had eyed each other like a couple of wary puppies over the restaurant table, and while Emma was quiet and polite, Desma seemed to have an air of well-cultivated boredom.

During the film, a romantic comedy rated suitable for family viewing, they sat together between the two adults, and although they laughed at the comic incidents, when Julian enquired afterwards if they'd enjoyed it, Emma said without enthusiasm, 'Yes, thank you.'

Desma had shrugged. 'It was okay, I s'pose...'

As they parted, Julian's rueful eyes had met Lacey's. Well, they hadn't expected too much of this initial meeting. But at least it was a start.

Later Tully got back into his wetsuit for the main event of the day, a team competition involving a water-based obstacle course, makeshift rafts, and a great deal of skulduggery on the part of the contestants, including flour bombs, water pistols and even fire hoses. Tully and his crew survived by a combination of skill and cunning, unfairly disabling most of the opposition, whose craft were clearly less expertly designed. His team was one of only two remaining contenders heading neck and neck for the finish line to a deafening roar from the crowd when a swell from a motorised boat further out to sea hit the two rafts, which veered towards each other and collided, pitching several of their occupants into the sea.

Rescue boats were at hand in case of mishaps, but for a second or two Lacey's heart was in her mouth as she counted the heads bobbing in the water before identifying Tully's seal-sleek one.

Emma, who had been jumping up and down and squealing with excitement, fell quiet, and Lacey put a hand on her shoulder. 'Daddy's okay,' she said, looking down at her daughter's crestfallen face. 'And it doesn't matter if they don't win.'

She glanced back at the water and saw that some of his crew had clambered back on board the raft, but now she couldn't see Tully.

She searched the choppy water with her eyes, then returned her gaze to the raft in case she'd missed him. No, none of those on board had his tall, broad-shouldered leanness combined with his dark hair. And all of them were looking over the side at the water.

Where was he? Lacey's hand unconsciously tightened on Emma's delicate shoulder bones.

Then two heads broke the water close to one of the rescue boats, and the crowd murmured to each other and raised hands to shade their eyes and see better against the glinting sun as a limp form was hauled onto its deck. Blood trickled down a whitened face.

'That's Daddy!' Emma said excitedly.

Lacey's breath stopped, until she saw what Emma meant. Tully was still in the water, leaning on the gunwale for a few seconds, then lifting a hand to the men in the boat as he pushed himself away.

He swam back to the raft, and the two crews sorted themselves out and completed the race, Tully's coming in just barely ahead of the other.

Almost before they touched the sand he leapt off and, brushing aside well-wishers and congratulations, strode to where the rescue boat had come into shore, a couple of ambulance officers racing to meet it.

'Is the man all right?' Emma turned an anxious face to her mother.

'I don't know.' A knot of people was gathering, and she couldn't see what was going on.

An ambulance drove down near to the beach and the crowd fell back. There was a short pause before the vehicle went off, and then she saw Tully coming towards them.

Emma and Riria ran to meet him, and Lacey hurried along behind them.

'Is he badly hurt?' Lacey asked. 'What happened?'

'He must have banged his head as he went over. He blacked out for a few seconds but came round almost as soon as we got him into the boat. They've taken him to hospital for observation, but he'll most likely be fine.'

Emma said, 'You saved his life, didn't you, Daddy?'

Tully looked down at her and laughed. 'Not really. The rescue boats are there for that. I just helped a bit.'

Someone called his name, and he said, 'Sorry, they want me for the victory ceremony. Don't go away.'

Emma dragged Riria and Lacey after him to watch the team collect a gaudy trophy and a giant bottle of champagne that they showered all over each other and a good part of the crowd, who didn't seem to mind.

On the way home, they stopped by the injured man's home to make sure his wife knew what had happened and that she didn't need any help, then dropped off Riria.

After swinging the car into the drive and pulling on the brake, Tully put his hand momentarily over Lacey's. 'Thanks for coming with Emma.'

She gave a small gasp. 'Tully, you're frozen!'

'My hands are a bit chilled, maybe.'

His skin had felt icy against hers, although the car heater had been on. 'Come inside,' she said. 'I'll make you a hot drink.'

He looked faintly amused, but didn't argue. Emma was already out of the car and waiting on the step for Lacey to unlock the door.

'Would you like a warm bath?' Lacey asked him when they were all inside.

'Sounds tempting,' he admitted. She saw now that his face had a pinched look that was unlike him. He gave an involuntary shiver, and she said, 'Emma, fetch your father a towel from the airing cupboard—a big one. Go on,' she urged him. 'You know where the bathroom is.'

She switched on the electric jug before shedding her jacket and going to hang it in her bedroom. There was a heater in the hallway and she turned up the thermostat on her way back to the kitchen. Taking down the coffee jar, she paused at the sight of the whisky bottle pushed into the corner of the cupboard, then reached in and took it out.

She poured a generous shot into a glass, added minimal water, and made for the bathroom and tapped on the door. 'Can I come in?'

'Okay.'

She pushed open the door and found him lying back in the bath, his head turned enquiringly towards her. He had the tub half-filled with steaming water, but the scanty bubbles of soap on the surface weren't hiding anything.

'I didn't realise you were already in the bath,' she said, almost retreating, then changing her mind. That would be silly, and probably afford him some amusement. 'I thought you might like a whisky.' Fixing her eyes on his face, she advanced towards him and placed the glass in the hand he held out for it, then immediately backed away. 'Coffee will be ready when you've finished in here.'

'Thanks. You do know how to pamper a man, Lacey. You wouldn't care to scrub my back, would you?'

'No, I wouldn't!' She paused in the doorway.

He laughed. 'I didn't think so.' Lifting the glass to her, he took a sip and then looked back at her, still grinning, but his eyes were oddly speculative. 'Why the outrage? I haven't asked you to get in here with me...though it's an interesting thought.'

It was a smallish modern bath, he could only fit in it with knees bent, and she couldn't help her lips curving with amusement. 'Dream on. That bath is definitely not big enough for two.'

His eyes held hers, the lurking laughter still in them. 'You wanna bet? It depends on what we want to do in it.' His brows rose interrogatively, suggestively.

'*We* wanted to get warmed up,' she said tartly. 'And I can see *we* are feeling much better already.'

'Oh, I'm warmed up, all right,' he said. 'Getting quite hot, in fact. How about you?'

She cast him a withering look as she turned away. '*I* wasn't half-frozen.'

But as she pulled the door shut behind her she thought he said softly, 'No?'

It was only teasing, she told herself, trying to quell the warm flutter of excitement in her stomach. He couldn't help himself. She supposed she'd asked for it by entering the bathroom, but for heaven's sake, it had been just a friendly gesture...

She made soup followed by warmed leftovers that she dressed up by sprinkling cheese on top and putting the dish under the grill. Of course Tully stayed, and joined her in the living room afterwards for another leisurely coffee while Emma got ready for bed. He had lit the fire for her while she cooked dinner, and when he came back from tucking Emma in he squatted down and piled a few pieces of manuka logs in the grate.

Dusting his hands, he stood up and said, 'Do you mind if I get myself another cup of coffee?'

'Of course I don't mind. You can get one for me, too.'

When he came back she had the TV on a current affairs programme, and he said, 'Oh, yes—I meant to watch this.'

They sat side by side on the sofa because the TV was in the recess by the fireplace, and from the two chairs it was difficult to see the screen. They had shared other evenings like this, but the last thing she'd ever wanted was Tully feeling that he had to spend time with her from any sense of obligation or worse, pity. So she issued invitations sparingly, and only when he seemed to be at a loose end and rather obviously angling for one. He never stayed late but she frequently felt a sense of restless disappointment when he'd gone.

After the programme finished Lacey picked up the remote control and said, 'Shall I turn it off or is there something else you'd like to watch?'

When he didn't answer, she looked at him and saw that his eyes were closed, his lips slightly parted, his head resting in the corner of the sofa while he cradled the empty coffee cup in his hands. He didn't stir when she removed the cup, nor when she said his name.

He'd had a physically exhausting day, and added to that was some mental strain when his team-mate had gone missing and then been found to be injured.

She switched off the television, eased a cushion under Tully's head and contemplated him again. After a moment she bent to untie his sneakers, slipped them off, and hoisted his feet up onto the sofa. It was long and roomy, but he wouldn't be able to lie full length. However, he seemed comfortable enough at the moment.

Before going to bed she dropped a duvet over him. If he woke he could let himself out. Anyone as tired as that shouldn't be driving, anyway.

In the morning she peeked into the living room and saw the sofa was empty, the duvet on the floor. She would tidy up later, but now she had to get Emma off to school.

It wasn't until she was shooing Emma out the door, making sure she was part of the neighbourhood group who regularly walked to school together, that Lacey noticed the Peugeot still parked in the driveway.

'Why did Daddy leave his car here?' Emma asked.

'I don't know,' Lacey said. 'Maybe because he'd been drinking whisky and didn't think he should drive. Go on, Emma, you'll be late for school.'

Puzzled, she turned back into the house to find Tully standing—or rather, leaning—in the living room doorway, his hands clutching the jamb on either side.

'What time is it?' he asked hoarsely.

Closing the door, she moved towards him. 'Eight o'clock. I thought you'd gone.' He must have been sleeping on the floor in front of the sofa, wrapped in what she'd thought was the discarded duvet.

He muttered something, shook his head and winced, giving a low grunt of pain. 'I should be,' he said, removing his hands from the doorway.

He swayed, and Lacey hurried forward, automatically slipping her arms about his waist to support him.

Even through his shirt she could feel the heat of his skin. His cheeks were dark with colour, his eyes glazed, and his lips looked parched.

'You can't go anywhere like this!' she said.

'I'm decent,' he said. 'Perfectly.' His head drooped and she felt the rasp of his unshaven chin against her temple.

'You're sick. You'd better lie down again before you fall.'

He said with reasonable clarity, 'That sofa's too damn small.'

Her bedroom was the closest and had a double bed. Sometimes when Emma was unwell or had been going through a phase of having nightmares or restless sleep, she'd been allowed to share it. 'A bed,' she said, rapidly making the decision. 'In my room.'

He tried to straighten up but it was obviously an effort. 'All right,' he said indistinctly. 'For a while.'

As he lay back on the bed she said, '*You* didn't hit your head yesterday, did you?'

'No.'

'Are you sure?' Lacey persisted.

An irritated frown crossed his face. 'Yes, sure. I'm okay. Go to work...soon.'

He sank back into sleep, and she frowned down at him, then went to telephone her doctor.

He wasn't in yet, but the nurse suggested, 'Plenty of fluid, aspirin or paracetamol for the fever, and call us again if you're worried. There are a lot of nasty viruses about. The doctors are all very busy. If he turns blue around the mouth or has trouble breathing you could call an ambulance.'

After that she called Cleaver's and got Tully's secretary. 'He won't be in today, and probably not tomorrow, either,' she said. 'He's too ill to talk. If he has any arrangements you'd better cancel them. He's asleep right now, but I'll give you my number.'

She roused Tully enough to push a couple of pills down his throat and make him drink some water, then tidied up, left the doors of the bedroom and dining room open, and started work.

It was difficult to concentrate, but she managed to translate a dozen pages of handwritten notes into neat printed ones before she heard Tully blunder into the bathroom.

When he emerged, staggering, she helped him back to bed and fetched more pills.

He looked at them suspiciously. 'What're you giving me?'

'Arsenic,' she said calmly. 'Take them. You're not allergic to any drugs, are you?'

'Not that I know of. What the hell have I got?'

'I've no idea. If you give me your doctor's name I'll try to contact...him? Her? Mine's busy. The nurse says there are lots of nasty viruses about and if you get worse I can phone them again or call an ambulance.'

'Don't be melodramatic,' he rasped. 'I haven't been near a doctor in years.'

'Well, take these and maybe you won't need one now, either.' She put an experienced hand on his brow and said, 'You're not as hot as before. Are you feeling any better?'

'If I felt any worse I'd be telling you to call an undertaker, never mind the doctor.' He put a hand to his head, then took the pills from her hand and tossed them down with water.

'Now who's being melodramatic?' she enquired. 'Drink all of that. You need lots of fluid. I'll get some more while you're still awake, and you should drink as much of it as you can.'

Settling back on the pillows, he said, 'Yes, nurse.' With a faint grin he added, 'You'd look good in a starched white uniform. With one of those wide, tight belts.'

'Really? I'm afraid I'm too busy to indulge your deviant fantasies. Besides, I'm all out of starch.'

Tully gave a ghost of a laugh and closed his eyes.

When Emma came home Lacey explained the situation and warned her not to make too much noise. 'And I'll be sleeping in the spare bed in your room tonight,' she added.

Emma thought it was all rather fun, Lacey could see, although when Tully next woke, she stood solemnly in the doorway of the bedroom and told him she was sorry he was sick.

'Just don't come too close,' he warned. 'I don't want you catching this bug. And that goes for you too,' he added, looking at Lacey when Emma had run off. 'You'd better keep away from me.'

'It isn't plague,' she said. 'Anyway, you were leaning all over me this morning. It's probably too late.'

He groaned. 'You should have thrown me out last night.'

'If you'd told me you were sick, I might have.'

He looked at her and grinned slightly. 'No, you wouldn't. You're too soft for your own good, Lacey. I didn't know I was sick, then. I thought being cold and tired and achey was a result of being in and out of the water all day, combined with physical exertion. I figured I was out of condition.'

'You looked in pretty good condition to me last night.'

In the bath. Of course he knew. He looked at her as though she'd surprised him, as she had herself. She'd always been so careful not to flirt with Tully, not to give him any chance to breach the defences she had painstakingly erected against him.

His grin widened. 'Pity I'm not in any condition *now* to follow up on that remark, but I'll bear it in mind for future reference.'

'Don't bother,' she advised him, making a commendable recovery. 'I was just trying to cheer you up.'

'Yeah? You have a kind, kind heart,' he said.

She could see he didn't believe her.

CHAPTER FOUR

IN THE middle of the night Lacey woke. She didn't know why, but perhaps some sound had disturbed her. She groped at the bottom of the narrow bed for her woolly robe and slipped it on, feeling in the dark for her slippers and then going quietly down the short hallway.

In her own room she could see dimly the man in the bed, and the bedclothes that he'd flung aside. He wore only the underpants and T-shirt that she'd washed earlier and dried for him, and his bare legs were free of the coverings.

Quietly she crossed to the bed and gently drew the bedclothes over him. But as she made to step back a hand closed on hers, and she saw the gleam of his eyes in the darkness.

'Don't go,' he said.

'Do you want something?' she whispered. 'I'll get you some more pills.'

'Just stay with me.'

Was he awake? She looked again but his eyes seemed to be closed now. The hand curled about hers was dry and hot, as if his temperature had climbed again. She touched her other hand to his forehead, relieved to find it less burning than earlier, and slightly damp. Automatically she pushed back a silky lock of dark hair.

'Mm.' He stirred and mumbled but didn't let go her hand.

He was dreaming. She should just free herself and go. Instead she sat down on the bed, holding his hand in both of hers.

It seemed a long time before his grip slackened, and when she got up her feet were icy, despite the slippers, and her back ached. But Tully was sleeping peacefully and his skin felt cooler. Carefully she loosed her hand, and on impulse bent and brushed a light, fleeting kiss on his forehead before going back to Emma's bedroom.

In the morning he got to the bathroom and back, and then lay on the bed breathing hard. Lacey surveyed him and told him he'd better get back under the blankets, and he argued unconvincingly for about half a minute and then gave in.

By evening, his temperature was almost normal and he'd managed to have a shower, and shaved with a disposable razor that Lacey fished from the bathroom cupboard.

'Women use them too,' she said tartly when he directed a questioning look at her from under his brows.

He laughed and turned to the mirror over the basin as she left the room.

He said on emerging, 'I'll be fine, now.'

She looked at the hand that was gripping the edge of the kitchen doorway rather firmly, and said, 'I'm already cooking a meal for three. You'd better have it before you think about driving. It's ages since you ate anything.'

He came into the room and dropped heavily into a chair. 'That probably accounts for why I feel as though I'm full of wet cotton wool.'

'You should probably stay another night. It won't make much difference if you don't go home until morning, will it?'

'Thanks, but I've imposed on you long enough.'

'You weren't imposing. I wouldn't have sent a dog home feeling the way you were.'

'That's put me in my place.'

He watched her silently while she prepared the meal. Obviously he wasn't up to making conversation, but she wished he wouldn't follow her every move with that air

of intense concentration. What, she asked herself rather
crossly, was so fascinating about watching a woman
cook? She was glad when Emma joined them and began
chattering to her father.

The following morning he looked considerably better.
He offered Emma a lift to school that she accepted ec-
statically, and as she ran to get her bag he turned to
Lacey and said, 'Thanks. You've been very kind.'

Shrugging, she said, 'I'd have done it for anyone.'

His faint smile became slightly wry as he said, 'I believe it, but I'm grateful all the same.'

Emma came back, reached up to kiss her mother, and
scampered out to the car.

'I never did get my victory kiss,' Tully said. 'And I'd
better not claim it now, although I'm probably over the
infectious stage.'

'You are obviously recovering fast,' Lacey said
crushingly. 'I never promised you any victory kiss.
Champagne is all you get.'

He grinned down at her. 'Champagne doesn't
compare. But I'll take a rain check.'

He was gone before she could argue, swinging away
from her and down the steps to join Emma. She thought
he was still smiling as he backed out the car.

Why had Tully taken to overtly flirting with her?
Except to remind Lacey on increasingly rare occasions
that he'd marry her if she wanted it, Tully had never
shown a real desire to initiate a closer bond—well, once,
she acknowledged.

Shortly after she and Emma had moved into the house
Tully bought for them, Lacey had invited him for a
special celebration dinner. Instead of the jeans or cotton
skirts she usually wore, she'd put on a flowered dress
with a wide neckline that showed off her creamy
shoulders. High-heeled shoes emphasised the slimness
of her ankles below the firm curves of her legs, and she'd

even found the floral perfume her sister had sent her for Christmas, and sprayed it on her skin.

Tully had brought a bunch of flowers, and a bottle of champagne that afterwards they'd finished off sitting side by side on the steps of the small back porch while Emma slept. It was a warm spring night, with a round yellow moon rising above the nearby houses. A wide, spreading plum tree laden with blossom grew in a corner of the back lawn, its branches silhouetted by the moonlight.

Lacey sat with her back to a post on the top step, and Tully one step below, facing her while they talked quietly.

'Do you miss your parents?' he asked her.

'Sometimes. It's nice having a place of our own, though. I am grateful, Tully.'

He moved restlessly. 'You have nothing to be grateful to me for.'

She did though, Lacey thought. She was grateful for Emma, although they'd certainly never planned to have a baby. But expressing her thanks always made Tully uncomfortable. She smiled at him and tipped her glass, draining the last of her champagne. 'The house is just right for us. And I love the plum tree.'

'The previous owners said it doesn't fruit well, it's too old. But I thought Emma will be able to climb it, and I could hang a swing for her on one of the branches.'

'She'd like that.' Lacey pictured him making it, his brown, capable hands fixing the ropes.

When Tully stood up to go, Lacey reluctantly rose and took the glass from his hand.

He leaned over and touched his lips briefly to her cheek. She smiled at him, feeling slightly mellow and muzzy, and he paused, his face in shadow so she couldn't see his expression. Instead of drawing back, he lowered his head again, his lips settling gently on hers.

She expected him to leave it at that, a simple goodnight kiss, but as his mouth lingered and subtly questioned, explored, she knew that whatever he had intended, this goodnight kiss had somehow turned into much more.

He wasn't touching her, and she stood with a champagne flute in each hand, almost afraid to move, a rising spiral of warmth and sweetness invading her body.

After a while she felt him take the glasses from her, heard the faint clink of the crystal as he put them down on the porch railing, and then he took her hands and placed them at his neck, before sliding his arms about her waist to pull her close to him.

When she wound her arms about his neck and kissed him back, he made the kiss deeper, harder, more demanding, until she trembled, small hot shivers of excitement running through her body, along her limbs.

After a while, still kissing her, he began to urge her slowly through the open doorway and along the darkened passageway into her new bedroom.

And there, as he bent to thrust back the bedspread, she dimly saw the photo of her parents sitting on the table by the bed, and went instantly cold, recalling something her father had said when she told him and her mother of Tully's plan to buy a house. 'He's not setting you up in order to have a convenient mistress, is he?'

She'd said vehemently it was no such thing, indignant that he should have thought so, and also well aware that if Tully wanted a 'mistress' he'd probably choose someone a lot more glamorous. But now the words came back to her with obscene clarity, freezing her blood. The possibility that her father was right seemed all too likely, and she felt sick with humiliation.

She pulled away, lost her balance and landed on the bed. Tully followed, his warm body trapping her, and she felt his hand at the front of her dress, opening the buttons, his fingers grazing her skin.

'No!' She fought away from him and stood up, clutching the edges of the bodice together and trying to catch her breath.

And when he sat up, demanding to know what was wrong, she choked out, 'Buying us a house doesn't mean I'm available to you for sexual favours whenever you're between girlfriends!'

He denied it, of course, furiously. But confronted with her scathing scepticism, he eventually flung at her, 'All right, believe what you want to! Crawl back into your frigid little shell!' And left in a towering temper.

He hadn't visited then for several weeks. When he did knock on the door, asking to see Emma, she thought he half expected her to deny him. His face was a taut mask of indifference bordering on hostility, but with a hint of the same stubborn determination she'd seen the day he'd found out she was pregnant and come round to suggest they get married. 'Are you going to let me in?' he asked.

Of course she had let him in. 'Emma's missed you,' she told him, and held the door wide. She thought the expression that softened his features then was relief, before Emma came running to fling herself into his arms.

They'd thrust that episode aside, keeping up the fragile facade of their delicate relationship for Emma's sake, but Lacey had never forgotten that night. And she knew he hadn't forgotten, either. Sometimes when she caught him watching her with a brooding, almost angry expression, she thought he had never been able to quite forgive her rejection of him.

Pushing the memory aside, she closed the door and went to wash the breakfast dishes, hugging herself against a sudden chill.

The chill passed off although she found herself fighting fatigue probably caused, she guessed, by the interrupted nights she'd spent looking after Tully.

The next morning her head ached slightly, and the day seemed particularly cold. She decided to indulge herself and switch on the heater in her office before starting work.

Naggingly, the headache persisted, and she couldn't stop shivering. By lunchtime she had to admit to herself that Tully's circumspection about infecting her had come too late. When Emma arrived home she found her mother huddled on the sofa with a duvet and hot water bottle.

'Don't come near me,' Lacey instructed her. 'You're going to stay with Mrs Dillon for a couple of days.' Their elderly neighbour occasionally acted as baby-sitter and she was fond of Emma. 'I want you to pack some things and then go over to her place. She's expecting you.'

'Who's going to look after you?' Emma queried.

'I'll be all right. Mrs Dillon's been in and she said she'd come back later and see how I am.' The older woman had insisted on leaving some chicken soup and made her promise to call on her if she needed help, but Lacey's only concern was that Emma was safely out of the way. She hoped it wasn't too late. Reassuringly she added, 'I've only got what Daddy had, and he's fine now. Only there's no reason why you should get it, too. You do feel okay, don't you?'

Emma confirmed it, and reluctantly did as she was told. Sighing with relief as she heard the back door close behind her daughter, Lacey reached for the bottle of pills on the floor and shook two into her chilled and trembling hand.

When she heard the door open again some time later she expected Mrs Dillon. The room had darkened and she felt groggy and hot, although her feet were icy.

She heard footsteps going towards her bedroom, and then a voice called, 'Lacey?' That was definitely not Mrs Dillon. 'Lacey, where the hell are you?'

She struggled up just as a bulky shadow filled the doorway.

'Lacey—I thought you'd be in bed. Sorry, did I wake you up?'

'Tully. What on earth are you doing here?'

'Emma phoned me, said you'd got my bug.' He was standing over her now, and she subsided back onto the cushions, her head throbbing mightily. 'She's worried about you, and so is Mrs Dillon. The poor woman's torn between concern for you and fear of infecting Emma.'

'If I don't have Emma to worry about I can manage on my own.'

'Not if you feel like I did, you won't. What are you doing here when you're ill?'

'I hate being in bed in the daytime.' It seemed like giving in, and Lacey seldom succumbed to sickness.

'It isn't daytime now. I'll help you into bed. I told Mrs Dillon I'll take over here.'

'You?' She would have laughed, only her head hurt too much. And her chest, and the rest of her.

'Tit for tat. Besides, I have a guilty conscience. You wouldn't be like this if I hadn't passed it on to you.'

'I don't see you as a nurse,' she objected. 'Just leave me alone, Tully. It'll all be over in a day or two.'

She might as well have saved her breath.

He proved to be a better nurse than she could ever have imagined. He fed her pills, even through the night, heated Mrs Dillon's soup and almost forced her to have some, was at hand with cool drinks every time she surfaced from feverish sleep, and sponged her down with lukewarm water before helping her into her nightgown, quelling her feeble protests with a curt, 'Don't be silly, Lacey. You're incapable of doing it yourself, and I'm not kinky enough to find the idea of ravishing a sick woman enticing.'

That wasn't exactly what she'd been worried about, but she found it too complicated to explain, and besides, the damp face-cloth on her overheated skin was wonderfully refreshing, so she gave up and just closed her eyes while he finished the task.

At one stage she surfaced groggily to find a vase of inexpertly arranged flowers swimming into her vision on the table by the bed.

'Did Emma pick them?' she asked Tully next time he came into the room. He seemed to have a sixth sense about when she was awake.

'No, I did,' he said. 'I thought they might cheer you up. I couldn't go out to buy flowers, so I raided your garden.' He twitched at a daisy that seemed determined to turn its face to the wall. 'I'm no florist, I'm afraid.'

'They're lovely,' she said weakly. So there were some things Tully couldn't do. But she was warmed by the fact that he'd thought of flowers for her.

On the third day, feeling blessedly cooler and less sick, although as weak as a starving kitten, she said, 'I take it all back. You missed your vocation. But really, you needn't have...'

'I owed you,' he reminded her, placing a tray holding toast and orange juice on her knees in the bed. 'Besides, it salved my conscience about giving it to you in the first place. Can you eat that now?'

Surprisingly, she found she could. 'Are there messages for me?' she asked him as he took the tray. She'd heard the phone ring and been profoundly thankful that there was someone else there to deal with it.

'A couple of your clients phoned. I told them if it was urgent to get someone else, but they both said they'll wait. And your friend Sally rang. I promised I'd let her know how you were.'

Lacey nodded. 'I'll ring her back myself.' Sally was her closest friend. She had three children, the middle one the same age as Emma.

'When I told her you were sick she wanted to know if she could help but I said everything's okay. Oh, and Julian rang.'

'Julian? Was he...surprised to find you here?'

'You could say that.'

'You did explain, didn't you?' She eyed him rather suspiciously.

'I explained. Don't worry, he isn't under the impression that you and I have been having wild erotic sex behind his back.'

Lacey brushed that aside. 'What did he say?'

'He said,' Tully repeated rather woodenly, 'that he was sorry you were sick, and if he didn't have Desma to worry about he'd have come over. And he'll see you when you're better.'

A faint disappointment warred with reason. Of course Julian didn't want to run any risk of passing this ghastly thing on to Desma. Hadn't her own uppermost thought been to protect Emma? And he couldn't have left Desma in order to nurse Lacey. It was easy for Tully, who had no domestic ties.

When she opened the mail that Tully handed her she found a Get Well card from Julian, which she propped on her bedside table. Later he phoned, and Tully brought the telephone in to her, then left the room and closed the door behind him.

'I'm feeling a lot better,' she assured Julian. 'Thank you for the card.'

'I wish I could have done more. Is Tully good at that sort of thing?'

'Surprisingly,' she said. But then, Tully was good at most things he put his hand to. It was something to do with never entertaining the possibility of failure, she suspected.

'I'd have thought if he wanted to help he'd have got in a nurse for you.'

'It wasn't necessary, really. He just didn't think I should be alone.' She shied away from detailing just how much Tully had done for her.

'Well, it was kind of him. I told him I appreciate knowing you're being looked after.'

Lacey blinked, opened her mouth and closed it again. She couldn't imagine what Tully had made of that.

'Are you there?' Julian enquired sharply.

'Yes. Yes...'

'I expect you're tired. Just take it easy for a while. I'll be in touch.'

She asked Tully, 'Don't you need to get back to work?'

'It's Saturday,' he said, and she realised she'd lost count of time. 'Anyway, I had my secretary bring over some paperwork and I've been in touch by phone. There's no hurry. I want to be sure you're fit and on your feet.'

She was, the next day, and proved it by getting up and showering without help. As she pulled off her nightgown, it crossed her mind that Tully wouldn't have found any of her nightwear in the least seductive. Just as well too, she reflected, as she stepped under the shower. She ought to think about buying something that was less of a passion-killer before her wedding day.

She sat up and watched television while Tully scribbled over a folder full of papers, and he made her a hot drink before she went back to bed.

On Monday morning when she came out dressed in a woolly jersey and corduroy pants, her newly shampooed hair still damp, Tully had breakfast ready in the kitchen.

She wasn't particularly hungry, but she ate a piece of toast and drank some of the coffee he'd made. And then said firmly that she really didn't need coddling any more and he must go.

He put down his cup and said, 'I'll wash up first. And don't try to do too much today. I'll call in later and see how you are.'

She knew it would be no use arguing. When he was shrugging into his jacket she said, 'You really have been terrific, Tully. I don't know how to thank you.'

He looked up, his eyes laughing. 'I can think of a couple of ways,' he said, coming towards her, 'but unfortunately I don't think you're up to them yet.' He dropped a light kiss on her lips, and as she made to move away his arm came around her waist and he pulled her against him. 'Keep still,' he muttered, and then he was kissing her properly, taking his time, his lips knowing and infinitely skilful as they parted hers.

He hadn't zipped his jacket and she could feel the warmth and hardness of his body even through his shirt and her woollen sweater. He felt good, and his arms were strong as he held her. She stayed in their seductive circle and didn't resist. Despite its decisiveness, his mouth was gentle on hers, promising rather than demanding, and the strength of his embrace made her feel not defenceless but ... cherished.

When he raised his head at last, his eyes lazily smiling into hers, she remained where she was for a moment before lifting her hands to push against his chest.

The smile spread to his mouth as he released her and turned away, closing the zip of his jacket.

He'd taken advantage of her weakness, she told herself. If she hadn't just been recovering from being ill he wouldn't have found her so compliant, or left her feeling so hot and breathless.

He was on his way to the door, but as he opened it he turned his head. He looked at her and let his eyes slip over her and it was like a caress, like being held again in his arms. Then, still smiling, he shook his head slightly and left without saying another word.

Damn, she thought. *Damn*! It didn't mean anything, it was just a thank you that he'd felt entitled to take from her. He wouldn't have read any more into it than that.

Julian had kissed her with more passion and surely no less finesse, and yet...

She almost felt as if her fever was returning.

At twelve-thirty the telephone on her desk rang.

'Lacey?' Tully's voice said. 'Have you had lunch?'

'I was just about to,' she lied. She'd been working all morning and hadn't looked at the clock.

'There's some more of Mrs Dillon's soup in the fridge,' he said, 'and some cold chicken.'

'Thanks, I'll find them.'

'I'll see you later.'

'There's no need, really—'

But he had already hung up.

After eating, she worked for another hour or so and then found she was drooping in her chair. She began making mistakes, her fingers faltering on the keyboard. Eventually she gave up and went to her room for a rest. Promising herself thirty minutes, she soon dropped off, sleeping until Emma arrived home from school and Mrs Dillon came over to check that Lacey was back to normal.

'Everything's fine, now,' Lacey assured her. 'I'm so grateful to you for looking after Emma.'

'She's been as good as gold,' the older woman said, smiling. 'And your Mr Cleaver, he's very nice, isn't he? You're lucky to have him.'

Lacey returned what she was afraid was a rather enigmatic smile. Tully's effect on women didn't fade with a woman's age, obviously.

He phoned again just as she was wondering what to make for the evening meal. 'Don't cook,' he ordered. 'I'll bring something. Do you fancy anything in particular?'

'Takeaways? I can't think of anything.' The prospect of chips or pizza wasn't particularly appetising.

But what he brought was a full meal of lean roast pork with vegetables, and she found herself enjoying it just as much as Emma did.

Pushing his own empty plate away, Tully watched her finish hers and gave a nod of satisfaction. 'Good?' he asked.

'Wonderful,' she told him. 'Thank you. I wasn't looking forward to cooking.'

'Care for some passionfruit cheesecake?'

'I'm not up to that yet. You and Emma are welcome to it.' Lacey started to get up, reaching for his plate.

Instead of giving it to her, he took a firm grip on her arm. 'You stay there. I'll do this.'

Slightly bemused by this unprecedented domestic side of Tully, she watched him clear the plates away and serve dessert for himself and Emma, then was towed to the lounge by her daughter to sit on the sofa while the two of them washed up. Tully had lit the fire earlier, and she sat watching the flames and feeling deliciously warm and satisfied.

She heard the phone ring and stop, and then Emma came in with the portable receiver and handed it to her mother.

'I hope you're feeling better?' Julian enquired. 'Emma said you're out of bed.'

'Yes, I'm fine now.'

'Great, I'm glad to hear it. How about having dinner with me tomorrow night, to celebrate?'

Lacey hesitated. Perhaps tomorrow was a bit soon. 'Could we make it Wednesday?'

'If that's what you'd prefer, of course.'

'I'll have to find a baby-sitter.' Could she ask Mrs Dillon again, after leaving Emma with her for several days? Maybe the teenager across the road...

'I could ask Desma to do it,' Julian offered. 'Perhaps the girls could get to know each other a bit better, without us around.'

He might have a point there. 'Well . . . I suppose you could ask her.' Lacey stifled the small doubt. It would probably work out just fine.

When Julian had cheerfully said goodbye, she switched the phone off and decided not to mention the arrangement to Emma until Julian had Desma's agreement.

'You're looking thoughtful,' Tully said, coming into the room with an armload of wood that he tipped into the basket by the fire, pausing to brush down his dark wool jersey. 'Problems?'

Lacey shook her head. 'No,' she said brightly. 'Not at all.'

'I'll put that back for you,' he suggested, taking the telephone from her hand. 'Unless you want to keep it by you?'

'Not specially.' She wasn't expecting more calls tonight. 'What's Emma doing?'

'Homework. I promised I'd give her a hand. Anything I can get for you? Help you into bed?'

She looked up quickly, but there was no teasing light in his eyes.

'I don't need help any more, thanks. I'll just watch some TV for a while.' But there was no programme that really interested her, and she soon switched off.

Tully came back and stooped to feed another piece of wood to the fire. 'I promised Emma I'd stay and tuck her in. She's in the bathroom now.'

'You're very good with her,' Lacey said warmly. 'Haven't you ever—?'

When she stopped herself he looked at her enquiringly. 'Ever what?'

'Ever. . . wanted to have a proper family. A wife, more children?'

He looked faintly startled, and then his eyelids came down a little, hiding the expression in his eyes. He hitched a shoulder against the mantelpiece and thrust his hands into the pockets of his charcoal wool pants. 'Is that what you meant when you said you planned to marry Julian because you want a "proper" family?'

Had he said 'planned to' or 'plan to'? She wasn't sure, and it took a split second to decide not to ask. Syntax wasn't the issue. 'I suppose that's part of it—' she began cautiously.

'How big a part?' he demanded. He was still leaning on the mantel, but she had the impression that his whole body had tensed. His voice deep, he said, '*I* could give you more children, Lacey... if that's what you want.'

She stared at him, and felt herself go hot and electrified, her body reacting to the suggestion in a purely sexual way that stunned her, her mind playing back to her a memory that she'd resolutely kept at bay for years. Tully at nineteen, leaning over her, his arms tight around her and eyes burning with passion, his young face pale and intent and his voice hoarsely, urgently inquiring, 'I'm not hurting you, am I? I don't want to hurt you. I... oh God! You are so lovely, so... sweet...' And then his mouth on hers, eager, searching, almost desperate.

Lovely, he'd called her, just that once. Her mouth twisted ironically. The light had been very dim, and it was amazing how a raw, adolescent hunger for sex could distort reality.

'Why are you looking like that?' He'd straightened, although he still had his hands hidden in his pockets. For a moment she was afraid that he had discerned her physical reactions, but his gaze was almost angry as he said, 'You've already had one child by me.'

'Yes, but...' She didn't know what to say. What on earth did he *want* her to say! He surely wasn't proposing to father a brood of extra-marital children? It was true that several times he'd suggested marriage, but always as a matter of expediency, a safety net for her or a balm for his own conscience. She was fairly sure that each time she'd refused his chief emotion had been relief.

'But?' he prompted her harshly.

'It isn't just a matter of having babies,' she tried to explain. 'It's spending my life with someone who cares—'

'*I* care! What the hell do you think I've been doing this past week? What have I done for the past ten years?' He glared at her, then swung away to walk a few paces and come back. 'You are my family,' he said. 'You and Emma.'

'I'm not your wife, Tully!'

'Your choice,' he said, his voice clipped. 'You've known all along you have only to say the word.'

'Yes, well, that's very chivalrous of you, but I also know you'd go into a blind panic if I ever did say it.'

He seemed to stiffen. His brows drew thunderously together and he took a step towards her, his hands leaving his pockets. 'The trouble with you is—'

And then Emma's voice interrupted as she came into the room, dressed in her pyjamas. 'I'm ready, Daddy.'

Tully straightened immediately, the fury leaving his face as Emma came to kiss Lacey goodnight.

'Goodnight, darling.' Lacey hugged her, glad of the distraction. She watched the two of them leave the room hand in hand, and felt a pang of some complicated emotion compounded of love and pain and uncertainty.

You are my family, you and Emma.

She put a hand to her head as a faint throbbing began in her temples. Sometimes life was too complicated. She had a sudden forlorn wish for Julian's calming presence. When she was with him she didn't suffer from the disturbing tensions of her relationship with Tully. She'd never felt the need to protect herself from getting too close to Julian, or been afraid that her emotions would swamp her reason.

Their love was a solid base for marriage, something that had grown gradually and was the stronger for it, and it certainly didn't lack a sexual component. That had its place, and its time. When the time was right she

was confident that they would find everything they expected in each other. Mature sex, after all, was a matter
of natural instinct and loving commitment. She and
Julian weren't heedless teenagers.

CHAPTER FIVE

'WHAT are you thinking about?' Tully had come back and was standing beside the sofa.

'Julian.'

She sensed his instant tension and looked up at him. His expression gave away nothing. The pounding at her temples intensified, and she instinctively rubbed at them.

'What's the matter?' Tully asked.

'Bit of a headache,' she murmured. 'It's nothing much.' She dropped her hand.

'You still look a bit pale,' he said critically. Stooping forward, he caught at her hands, drawing her to her feet. 'You'd better have an early night. Is there anything you want before I go?'

Lacey shook her head, grateful that he seemed to have conquered his earlier spurt of temper. 'No, you've done more than enough. Thank you again, Tully.'

His eyes searched hers, and she made to pull away her hands, remembering his insistence on a kiss last time.

'I've never figured out,' he said, releasing her, 'why you ever let me make love to you.'

Lacey said crisply, 'I was young and silly and we'd both been drinking.'

'And that was enough?'

She cast him a look of deliberate mockery. 'Tully, you must know all the girls thought you were God's gift.' Even at nineteen he'd been special, with his dark, youthful good looks and confident air, and a smile that could melt female teenage hearts at twenty paces.

He looked almost startled. 'No,' he said slowly, 'I didn't know that. I guess I was too wrapped up in—'

He stopped, and she supplied dryly, 'Francine. I know.'

His eyes went slightly glazed, and his lips curved, obviously at a recalled memory. 'Francine,' he agreed. 'What a little minx your sister was.'

Lacey didn't dispute it. They might have been made for each other, Francine and Tully. Two beautiful young people, both thinking the world was their oyster, both spirited, more than a bit spoilt, and fond of their own way. Everyone had thought they made a perfect couple. And everyone had been stunned that it was Francine's quiet, ordinary, and dumpy younger sister who had come between them.

Not least Francine herself. Lacey still remembered with wincing clarity the hysterical scenes Francine had created when Lacey confessed to their shocked parents that she was pregnant with Tully's child.

'After all,' Tully said, cutting into her reflections, 'you'd made it pretty clear that you didn't even like me.'

'*Like* you?' Lacey gave him a rueful smile. 'No, I never liked you, Tully.' She'd found him too handsome, too clever, too sure of himself, too...everything. But she hadn't been unaware of the reason why Francine and all the other girls in their circle found him exciting.

Sullenly, she'd made up her mind not to like him. He might make her skin prickle with pleasurable warmth, and send the blood singing in her veins, and turn her knees to mush, but even at barely seventeen she'd perceived that for what it was—a purely physical, animalistic response to a potent, if largely unconscious male sexuality.

Francine had responded to it like a bee scenting nectar, and like the bee, as Tully later discovered, Francine could sting when she wanted. But Lacey had been hostile from the first time she saw him. Recognising danger, she had reacted with a mixture of fear, fascination and loathing.

Until that summer's night when everything had changed. What had happened was, she supposed, inevitable, given their youth and the circumstances and their mutual stupidity.

The repercussions had been horrendous. Francine had been beside herself with fury and, Lacey supposed, grief. She'd certainly cried up a storm, between screaming at her sister and threatening to leave home if Lacey didn't, and phoning Tully to alternately weep and call both him and Lacey vicious names.

Possibly it was their parents who'd had the worst of it, Lacey thought. Trying to support both daughters and reconcile them, they'd been inclined to blame Tully for the whole sorry mess. But that was the one thing in which Lacey and Francine had been united. Tully wasn't to blame. Neither of them would allow him to be forced to take responsibility.

He hadn't needed to be forced, though. He'd arrived at the door looking white but determined, and asked to speak to Lacey alone, his eyes resolutely avoiding Francine's pinched and tear-stained face, her starkly accusing gaze, and the sodden handkerchief clasped in her restless hands. And when the girls' parents had left the room, taking a reluctant Francine with them, he'd asked Lacey to marry him.

It had been hard, but thank God she'd had the sense to refuse. Even then, frightened and worried and guilt-ridden as she was, she'd known that marrying Tully would only have compounded the disaster.

He'd tried to hide his relief when she turned him down. He'd even tried, valiantly, to persuade her to change her mind, asked her if she shouldn't consult her parents, but she'd held firm. Nothing would make her marry Tully.

And nothing that had happened since had led her to regret that decision.

'You don't still dislike me, do you?' he asked her.

Lacey shook her head. 'No, of course I don't dislike you, Tully. You've been great with Emma, and very kind to me.'

'That isn't kindness,' he said. He was looking at her as though debating something inside himself. 'You know it isn't.'

His generosity had sprung, no doubt, from a sense of obligation. But he loved Emma, and over the years she supposed he'd developed a careless fondness for Lacey.

'I value your friendship,' she offered.

'Friendship?' Something flickered in his eyes and was gone. She tensed as he bent forward, but he only brushed her forehead with his lips and said, 'Goodnight, Lacey. Go to bed.' He swung away to the door and she heard him let himself out.

Desma had agreed to stay with Emma on Wednesday evening, Julian reported. 'She needed hardly any persuasion,' he said. 'I suspect she liked Emma better than she's letting on.'

Lacey couldn't fool herself that the feeling was mutual. When she told Emma the little girl's face took on a mutinous look. 'Why do I have to have *her* looking after me? Why do you want to go out to dinner with Julian, anyway?'

'Because Julian would like to do something nice for me, to make up for my being sick. And...' Lacey added carefully '...because we enjoy going out together.'

Emma gave her a belligerent stare. 'Parents aren't supposed to leave their kids alone.'

Lacey smiled. 'That's why Desma's going to stay with you, because I want to be sure you're looked after while I'm out.' She paused. 'You've never minded staying home with Mrs Dillon or Lindy to look after you.'

'That's different. Desma's a *stranger*.'

'She's not a stranger,' Lacey said, squashing a tiny inner voice that told her she didn't know Desma very well. The girl was Julian's daughter and he was sure she was capable.

Desma seemed willing if not anxious to make a good impression when she arrived with her father. Julian was obviously pleased when she held out her hand and said, 'It's nice to see you again, Ms Kerr.'

'And you,' Lacey said, slightly amused at the formality. 'Do call me Lacey if you like. Emma's in the bath but she'll be out soon. I've left biscuits and fruit on the table for you.' She'd also left an envelope with Desma's name on it and some money inside, guessing that Julian might feel Desma should refuse payment. 'And there's orange juice in the fridge, but if you want coffee, tea, cocoa...'

'Thanks. I'll find them. What time will you be back?'

'Before eleven,' Julian promised.

Emma came in, regarding them all with a slightly wary stare. 'I want Mummy to tuck me in,' she announced.

For months she'd been calling Lacey 'Mum' except on the odd occasion when she reverted, but Lacey had the feeling that this time the more childish version was quite deliberate.

'Wouldn't you like to keep Desma company for a while?' she suggested.

Emma shook her head. 'I want to read my book.'

'I'll read you a story if you like,' Desma offered.

Turning her gaze to the older girl, Emma said politely but very positively, 'I can read it myself, thank you.'

'Okay.' Desma dropped into a chair, turning her gaze to the television and video player in the corner. 'I brought some music videos. Is it okay if I play them?' she asked Lacey.

Lacey gave permission, handed her the remote control and followed Emma to her bedroom. 'You'll be good, for Desma, won't you?' she urged. 'It was nice of her to say she'd read to you.'

'I'm too old for that.'

It wasn't so long since she'd requested the service of her father, but Lacey let that pass. No doubt that had been an excuse to keep him with her a bit longer. 'I'm going to tell her you have to turn off your light at half past eight.'

Emma hunched down against the pillows. 'Yeah, okay.' She opened her book.

The evening went pleasantly enough, and Lacey told herself that her vague feeling of ennui was the aftermath of the virus. Julian was attentive and considerate, the food well presented and the restaurant obviously popular, but the buzz of conversation about them brought back the slight headache that had plagued her on and off since her recovery.

She tried to shed a faint, irrational unease about Emma, but when Julian suggested a second cup of coffee after the meal she declined, willing him to quickly finish his.

He was in no hurry, however. 'This is nice,' he said, resting a hand on hers where it lay on the table. 'It seems ages since I had you to myself.'

'Does it? Yes, it is nice,' she agreed, mustering a smile for him. 'It was sweet of you to think of it.'

'My pleasure,' Julian said warmly. 'We should do this more often. Perhaps Desma will baby-sit again.'

'Maybe. But she's reached the age where she'll want to be going out herself at the weekends. What about her boyfriend?'

'That's over, thank heaven. He wasn't really her type at all.'

'There'll be others.'

'Oh, sure, but as I told her, there's plenty of time for that sort of thing. I'd like to see her concentrate on her studies for a while.'

When they arrived back at the house, Julian pulled on the handbrake and turned to draw Lacey into his arms.

Her fingers already on the door handle, she relinquished it, returning his kiss. But somehow her senses remained unstirred, and when he started to unfasten her jacket she pulled away.

'What is it?' he asked.

'I don't know,' she confessed. 'Maybe it's because Desma's here.'

He laughed a little. 'I know what you mean. I think parents possibly have a greater fear of being caught necking by their teenage children than the other way round.'

Inside, they found Desma watching a noisy music video. She didn't even notice their presence until her father walked over to the TV set and turned down the sound.

'Oh, hi,' she said. 'Have a good time?'

'Lovely, thank you,' Lacey said quickly, noticing signs of parental displeasure in Julian's face. 'Is everything all right?'

'Yeah, Emma's asleep—'

'Through *that*?' Julian asked sceptically.

'I closed her door,' Desma said virtuously. 'She's okay, honest. I checked on her and everything.'

Lacey stopped herself from going to check, herself. 'I hope you enjoyed yourself—' puzzled at Desma's faintly startled look, she added '—listening to your music.' From Julian's pained expression she guessed that Desma didn't often get a chance to play hours of it on high volume.

'Oh—yeah. Yes, thank you.' Desma smiled at her suddenly. 'Dad hates it. I had some biscuits and stuff,' she said, going over to remove the tape from the machine, 'and I've washed up.'

She wasn't a bad kid, Lacey told herself. She was putting herself out to be helpful.

As soon as Desma and Julian had gone she hurried down the passageway and softly opened the door to Emma's room.

She was fast asleep, just as Desma had said, and Ruffles, his chin resting on his paws, lay curled up against her. Lacey smiled down at the two of them, the child's dark hair cloudy on the white pillow, her lashes inky against her cheeks. The pale, smooth forehead and small, determined chin looked so vulnerable in sleep. Lacey unnecessarily straightened the sheet, and tiptoed out.

Emma didn't mention Desma at all the following day, and to Lacey's casual enquiry she said, 'She was all right.' Asked if the music had disturbed her, she said, 'I was asleep.'

Knowing that extolling the older girl's virtues ad nauseam or trying to wring a positive response from Emma would only antagonise the child, Lacey bit her tongue and hoped that in time Emma would come round.

Tully called to ask how Lacey was. 'I phoned last night,' he said.

Desma hadn't mentioned a caller. Perhaps she'd forgotten. 'I was out,' Lacey said.

'Yes. Who was the baby-sitter?'

'Julian's daughter.'

'Cosy. It was Julian you went out with, I presume.'

'That's right—what else do you want to know?'

'Sorry,' he said after a moment. 'Just showing an interest. Is it a secret?'

'Of course not. What do you want, Tully?'

'I told you, I wanted to be sure you're okay. I guess if you were well enough to go out on the town with the boyfriend I needn't have worried.'

'No, you needn't. And we weren't out on the town. We had dinner, that's all.'

'*All*?' he asked, a wealth of curiosity and suggestion in his voice. He was laughing at her.

Lacey gritted her teeth. 'Anything else,' she said reck-lessly, 'is none of your business.'

The silence on the line was loaded. 'Right.' The laughter had left his voice. 'I'll see you, then.' And he put down the receiver.

Emma seemed quieter than usual, so that Lacey won-dered if she'd not escaped the virus after all, but she cheered up when Tully phoned and asked her if she wanted to go riding again at the weekend.

When he came to fetch her Lacey was kneeling on the front lawn, pulling out weeds in a bed of creamy freesias that were just opening up.

'Are you well enough to be working like that?' Tully asked her.

She stood up, not enjoying the sensation of kneeling at his feet, and automatically stripped off one of her gardening gloves to push back her hair. 'I'm perfectly fit now.'

He ran his eyes over her baggy shirt and the threadbare jeans with holes in the knees. 'Not going out with Julian today?' he enquired.

Obviously she wasn't going anywhere dressed this way. 'The garden needs tidying up,' she said. She'd thought of asking Julian if he'd like to come and help, but she rather enjoyed doing the job on her own. There was something both soothing and satisfying about a quiet, solitary afternoon spent yanking out weeds.

'Daddy!' Emma came flying out of the house, her windbreaker half on, one sleeve dangling. 'I'm ready.'

'There's no hurry,' he said, and reached out to help her pull the jacket on as she came to his side. 'We won't be late,' he added to Lacey, his hand absently stroking Emma's hair. 'I'll tell you what, you'll be tired when you've finished that. Why don't we all go into town for dinner, save you cooking?'

'Oh, yes, please!' Emma said before Lacey could say anything. 'We haven't done that for ages! We can, can't we, Mum?'

Her first instinct was to say no, but with Emma's pleading eyes on her she didn't have the heart. And Tully was right, it would be a pleasant ending to the day, to have a good meal prepared by someone else. 'All right, that would be nice. Thank you,' she said.

As they went to the car she firmly pushed away a vaguely guilty feeling. Julian had suggested dinner tonight, but she'd turned it down on the grounds that they'd had one date this week already and she didn't want to leave Emma with a sitter again so soon.

This wasn't a date, and Julian would have no cause for complaint even if he was the jealous type, which he wasn't.

She and Tully had a friendly, flexible and very civilised arrangement. When Tully had first said that he would like some contact with Emma, just before her second birthday, Lacey had admittedly been rather cautious, but she'd thought it would be good for Emma to have contact with her father, even if the contact was sporadic and perhaps didn't last. He had graduated by then and left home, at the same time stepping into a junior management position in his father's business. He'd never said so, but she suspected that seeing Emma was part of some process of freeing himself from his mother, who had never acknowledged her grandchild.

It had crossed Lacey's mind that when the novelty wore off Tully might lose interest in his daughter, but she would always be there to provide stability, and she didn't think she had the right to deny him.

There had seemed no reason to invoke any legal processes, and there was no strict timetable. She didn't want Emma to have expectations that might be disappointed. The one rule she stipulated for Tully was that he would never make Emma a promise that might have to be broken.

She had perhaps underestimated Tully, she had to admit. Far from losing interest, he had spent more time with Emma as she got older. When she was little his visits had been intermittent, brief and often awkward. The awkwardness had probably been inevitable, given that for the first four years of Emma's life she and her mother had lived with Lacey's parents, who invariably gave Tully an icy reception.

They blamed him for seducing Lacey and for causing Francine to leave home. Probably the latter was the more unforgivable, Lacey thought. Her parents had stood by her, and she was grateful, but it had seemed more a matter of disappointed duty than love.

They couldn't help but become fond of Emma, and still sent her birthday and Christmas presents, but when Francine married a doctor and moved to Christchurch, where she produced twins—a boy and a girl—within six months they'd sold their home and gone to the South Island to be near her. 'After all,' they said to Lacey, 'with two babies, Francine can do with some help. And you've had your share—we've even given you and little Emma a home. Of course, you can come with us if you like. It's up to you.'

'No,' she said. 'I couldn't take Emma away from Tully now. I'll find something. It's probably time we moved out on our own, anyway.'

That was when Tully had insisted on buying a house for Lacey and Emma. By that time he'd taken over the management of Cleaver's in Auckland. 'I can afford it,' he'd told her, 'and I want to do it for Emma. You can't deprive her of a decent home because of your silly pride.'

So for Emma's sake she had accepted. And Tully's visits had become more frequent and lasted longer.

At Emma's fifth birthday party he'd taken photographs of the occasion with a Polaroid camera he had bought specially so that she and her friends could see the instant results. He'd acted like any proud father, and while Lacey cleaned up afterwards Emma perched on his knee and they re-examined all the pictures together. She giggled and chattered, and when he'd put away the photographs they'd sat on the floor for ages playing with her presents until Lacey decreed it was time for Emma's bath.

Once Emma was in the water Lacey returned to the lounge and began gathering up the wrapping paper, discarded boxes and toys strewn on the floor.

'Is the bath over?' Tully asked.

'No, I don't really bath her any more, I just supervise.' She picked up a jigsaw puzzle still in its Cellophane wrapper and dropped a piece of coloured paper.

Tully stooped and retrieved it for her. 'Here, give me the rubbish,' he said, removing the rest of the wrappings she'd collected from her grasp. 'Where do you want all this? In the kitchen bin?'

'Yes, thanks.' She made a neat pile of the presents and placed them in a corner, then flopped down on a chair.

She was still there when Emma came in, her pyjamas on and her skin glowing pink, and her precious stuffed rabbit—a huge toy almost as long as she was that Tully had given her on her third birthday—clasped in her arms.

'Did you clean your teeth?' Lacey asked.

'Yes, see?' Emma bared them at her. 'Grrr.' Tully had appeared in the doorway behind her, his expression amused and fascinated.

Emma pulled at Lacey's hand. 'Put me to bed, Mummy.'

'Yes, okay,' she said, stifling a yawn, and began reluctantly to get up.

'Will I do?' Tully asked, strolling forward. His eyes on Lacey, he added, 'Your mother's tired.'

'Are you tired, Mummy?' Emma asked.

Lacey smiled at her solemn expression. 'A bit.'

'Okay then.' She turned to tuck her hand into Tully's. 'You have to read me a story.'

Over her head, Lacey sent him an ironic glance.

'Fine,' he agreed. 'Just tell me which one...'

They left the room and Lacey closed her eyes. She didn't realise that Tully had returned until he spoke her name, very softly.

Her eyes flew open to find his face only inches from hers. He was smiling, and his hands were on the arms of the chair, trapping her.

'It's amazing,' he said. 'You look like Emma when you're asleep.'

'She's asleep already?'

'So have you been for the last ten minutes.'

'I wasn't!' She couldn't believe it.

'You were,' he contradicted her. 'I was tempted to use the classic method to wake you up.' His eyes asked a smiling, man-to-woman question, and her heart gave a thump in answer.

'Just as well you didn't,' she said tartly. 'You'd probably have got a classic slap in the face.'

The smile spread to his mouth, his expression quizzical in the extreme as he straightened and put his hands in his pockets, but didn't move away. 'Why?'

'I'm not accustomed to being woken with...'

'Kisses?' he supplied, the smile still tugging at his mouth.

'Unexpected—unwanted kisses.'

'Mm.' He looked at her thoughtfully. 'Which would it have been? Unexpected? Or unwanted?'

'Both,' she returned instantly. She stood up, assuming he would move back and leave room, but he didn't.

They were no more than a foot apart. He was looking quite sombre as his eyes searched her face. 'Do you hate me, Lacey?' he asked her.

Taken aback, she said, 'No, of course not! Why should I hate you?'

'I wrecked your life, didn't I?'

'My life isn't wrecked. It's just different from what I thought it would be.'

'Still,' he said, 'it's true that women get the worst of it. The fact is, I can walk away any time.'

'Do you want to walk away?' she asked him.

'No! Lacey...I meant it when I said I'd marry you. Any time you change your mind, just let me know.'

Lacey smiled, shaking her head. The ultimate sacrifice, she thought. But she was touched that he was willing to make it for Emma's sake. 'No,' she said. 'Let's leave things as they are. You've done more than you needed to already. The house is great, and Emma's very happy here.'

'What about you? Are you happy?'

'When Emma's happy, I am,' she told him. After a brief hesitation she asked, 'What's the matter, Tully? Woman trouble?'

'Why do you say that?' He sounded rather defensive.

Lacey shrugged. 'Call it intuition.' Of course he'd had several girlfriends since Francine. A couple of times he'd let names slip in casual conversation. And once she'd phoned his office about a small problem with the ownership papers on the house. His secretary had said pleasantly, 'He's busy right now. Perhaps I can help?'

'It's a personal matter,' Lacey explained.

'Oh, if that's Caroline,' the woman said warmly, 'he's expecting your call, I'll put you straight through.'

Before she had a chance to deny it, Tully's voice had come on the line, deep and vibrant and eager. 'Caro? Darling, I'm sor—'

'It's Lacey,' she interrupted quickly.

'Lacey?' he enquired blankly. 'Mrs Palmer said—'

'I know.' The woman's a fool! Lacey thought viciously. Why couldn't she have checked? 'She made a mistake.'

'Yes.' He sounded cool now, brisk. 'What can I do for you?'

After she'd explained the problem and he'd said he would take care of it, she rang off and fought a desire to kick something.

'Intuition?' Tully repeated. 'Why, what have I done that could lead your intuition to diagnose "woman trouble"?'

For one thing, he'd shown a faint interest in kissing Lacey, and an even fainter one in the idea of marrying her, but she didn't cite that. Instead she said, 'It's just a feeling I have.'

He gave a rather bitter little laugh and swung away from her. 'Well, it needn't concern you, anyway.'

Feeling rebuffed, she said, 'I only thought that if I could help in any way...'

Turning to face her again, he said with angry mockery, 'We've been down that road before, haven't we? How far are you willing to go this time? A minute ago you said my touch was unwelcome—what is it with you? Do you have to be feeling sorry for a man before you can sleep with him?'

Stunned at the sudden attack, Lacey recoiled. 'That isn't what I was suggesting, and you know it! I wouldn't sleep with you again for—for anything you can name!' The memory of how nearly and how recently she'd come close to breaking that resolution gave her denial extra vehemence.

'No, you wouldn't, would you?' he said unexpectedly. 'Not even for Emma.'

'Emma?'

'I asked you to marry me,' he said harshly. 'Or has it slipped your mind already? To give Emma a normal family life, with a mother and father living in the same house, sharing the same bed. And you turned me down without a second thought—again.'

Lacey almost laughed. He was annoyed because she repulsed his casual, almost mechanical pass at her and refused his off-handed proposal. 'I'm sorry,' she said automatically. 'I didn't mean to offend you.' Although she couldn't help thinking that she was the one who had a right to be offended, surely.

Tully scowled. 'You didn't *offend* me,' he said shortly. He passed a hand through his hair and, watching, Lacey had a disconcerting memory of how silky and cool it had felt in her fingers once, a long time ago... 'I'd better go,' he said. 'I don't think this conversation is getting us anywhere.'

Lacey could only agree. She saw him to the door, and fought an urge to smooth the crease that remained between his black brows. 'I hope it works out for you,' she said softly as he reached the steps outside.

He turned, surprise in his expression, and stared at her for a moment. Then his lips moved in a wry smile. 'Thanks,' he said, and carried on down the steps, taking a short cut across the lawn to his car.

Some months after that birthday party, Lacey found out that Tully's mother had remarried and moved to America with her new husband at about that time. His relationship with his mother had always seemed rather prickly and distant, and he had never been close to his father, who apparently only contacted him on business matters, but she wondered if deep down he'd felt abandoned, lonely, just as she did sometimes.

Her mother wrote once a week—short letters, mostly about Francine and the twins but also about the city of Christchurch, '...so nice and quiet compared to Auckland, and we've met such nice people.' And later she wrote about the bowling club she and her husband had joined and the plans they had for converting the garage into a spare room '...and if we get too feeble to manage the stairs we'll use it for our bedroom, so we don't have to leave our lovely little home.'

When Emma was seven Lacey had flown down to Christchurch with her in the school holidays and they had stayed for a week in the spare room. Emma had been wild with excitement at the prospect of meeting her cousins. She had always been fascinated by the photographs of the twins that accompanied some of her grandmother's letters.

Lacey's parents had greeted Emma fondly, and Francine had brought the twins to visit. Accustomed to having their grandparents' undivided attention, the younger children were put out by the fact that the toy cupboard they'd always regarded as theirs had been opened to this girl they had never met. The twins closed ranks in defence, declaring that they didn't like her, and while Lacey could understand that, her heart ached at Emma's bewildered disappointment.

Her parents tried to help by expressing their disapproval of such rude and inhospitable behaviour, urging the twins to 'share' and 'be nice to your cousin.' Both they and Francine interpreted that as a criticism and reacted defensively. Lacey took Emma aside and explained that the twins didn't understand that their grandparents were also hers, and were worried and insecure. 'When you all get to know each other maybe they'll feel better about you.'

Emma, trying to hide her tears, nodded solemnly and said in a doubtful voice that she understood, but from then on she clung to Lacey's side and said nothing.

Francine, although she had made some effort to express interest in Lacey's life in Auckland, had soon run out of things to say and talked mostly to her mother. As she was getting up to leave she said brightly, 'You must bring Lacey and Emma over one day. Maybe for lunch?'

But when they did the twins were away for the day. Lacey suspected that Francine had deliberately arranged it, and in a way she didn't blame her. That first meeting had been uncomfortable for all of them, and Francine must have felt embarrassed at her children's bad manners. It did seem a pity, though, if the children were never to be given a chance to discover if they could have got on better.

Her parents were kind and insisted on taking Emma and Lacey out every day to a park or the mountains or to see friends, but Lacey had the feeling that the visit was disrupting their normal routine and was a bit of a strain.

They had dinner one night with Francine and her husband Lloyd, a good-looking man with sandy hair and even, pleasant features. Emma sat in a corner of the TV room while the twins, who had been given their meal earlier, lay on cushions in front of the set and ignored her until it was time for them to go to bed.

Their father was pouring a second round of drinks for the adults when they besieged him for a story.

'Daddy's too busy for stories tonight,' Francine told them.

Her father put down the glass Lloyd had just handed him. 'I'll read to them,' he announced. 'Want to come, Emma?'

Her face brightening, Emma jumped up and trailed after them. When Francine asked Lacey to tell her father dinner was served, she found him sitting on one of the beds, and Emma snuggled on his knee. With glowing eyes and pink cheeks, she was reading aloud from the book he held while the twins listened, sleepy and content. Emma had always been a good reader, and already she could invest a text with vivid expression.

It was a picture Lacey cherished in her memory for a long time. Whenever she thought of it she felt a rush of gratitude to her father.

CHAPTER SIX

When Tully and Emma returned from riding Lacey was in the shower, washing away the dirt of her afternoon's gardening. With her hair roughly towelled dry and a bathrobe belted around her, she left the bathroom and found Tully standing just outside it.

'Where's Emma?' she asked him.

'In her room, changing her clothes. You smell nice.' He leaned forward and sniffed.

'Apple shampoo,' she said.

'Mm, you look delicious, too.'

'You don't have to turn on the charm for me, Tully. I'm immunised.' She made to walk past him to her bedroom, and he stepped back but laid a hand on the wall, blocking her with his outstretched arm. 'And you can stop playing games!' she snapped.

'*Games*?' he said softly.

'You know what I mean. Get out of the way.'

He looked at her with a thoughtful air, not moving. 'Please?' he suggested.

Lacey gritted her teeth. 'Please, Tully,' she said with heavy sarcasm, 'will you let me pass? And while you're about it,' she added, as he lazily stood aside and she covered the few steps to her room, 'will you please *grow up*!'

Slamming the door behind her relieved her feelings a little, but she still seethed as she jerked undone the belt of the robe and crossed swiftly to her dressing table. Dragging a comb through her wet hair, she cursed silently at every knot. She was still cursing as she put on underwear, belted herself into a flattering striped go-

anywhere dress and pushed her feet into medium-heeled
pumps. She stroked foundation quickly onto her face
and applied a dash of eyeshadow. Picking up a lipstick,
she dropped the cap trying to remove it, and had to wipe
off her first attempt and try again, because her hand was
shaking.

Damn Tully, *damn* him. He must have been doing this
to women since he was sixteen! All it needed was a look,
a smile, a teasing remark that meant nothing to him—
nothing, she reminded herself. It was simply the way he
related to all women, he couldn't help himself.

I'm immunised, she'd told him just now. Only it wasn't
true. There was no vaccination against what Tully
carried.

Still, for years she'd suppressed any covert response,
managed to erect some kind of barrier that protected her
from all but a mild, inescapable recognition of his unconscious magnetism. She'd set boundaries on their relationship and made them clear to Tully. He was Emma's
father but in no way was he Lacey's lover. She was always
pleasant and friendly but his every attempt at flirting
was met with a blank stare or a light evasion, and she
discouraged even the most casual touch.

And for years Tully had accepted those unspoken
limitations. They'd been almost comfortable with each
other, although maintaining the delicate balance had
been something of a strain on Lacey.

Lately Tully seemed to have been deliberately trying
to alter that balance. And she mustn't allow it.

She took her time over drying and brushing her hair,
not emerging from the bedroom until she heard Emma
talking to Tully.

When she appeared in the lounge doorway Tully shot
her a questioning glance which she avoided, smiling for
Emma's benefit as she announced brightly, 'I'm ready.'

He gave her an approving look that lingered a bit too
long, but he made no comment on her appearance.

They went to a Chinese restaurant, Chinese being Emma's favourite cuisine. To Lacey's relief she was perkier than she'd been for days, sharing dishes and, as the meal drew to a close, renewing her request for a horse.

'You know we haven't enough room for a horse,' Lacey reminded her patiently.

'We don't have to keep it at home! Lots of people rent land for grazing.'

'That's expensive. Owning a horse costs money, Emma, even apart from the cost of buying one.'

'Daddy's got money,' Emma announced. 'Haven't you, Daddy?'

Tully gave Lacey a rueful look and said, 'Yes, I have money.'

'You can't just expect Daddy to pay for everything you want,' Lacey told her rather sharply.

'Why?' she demanded. 'He *likes* buying things for me, don't you, Daddy?'

'Sure I do—'

'There!' Emma said triumphantly. 'You're just being *mean*—'

Lacey took a deep breath, but before she could say anything Tully cut in. 'That's enough, Emma!'

'But she *is*!' Emma insisted tragically. 'She's always saying things cost too much, she just won't let me have *anything*, and she hates you giving me things!'

'Emma,' Lacey began, shocked, 'I don't—'

'*Be quiet*, Emma!'

Stopped in mid-flow by the rare anger in Tully's voice, Emma stared at him, gulped and then dissolved in tears.

Tully looked from her to Lacey, who was as nonplussed as he. Emma's outburst had been uncharacteristic, and this was even more so. 'Maybe going out tonight wasn't such a good idea,' Lacey said.

'You see?' Emma choked. 'She doesn't want us to have a good time!' She scrubbed at the tears on her cheeks with her hands.

Tully scowled and opened his mouth to say something, but Lacey shook her head. 'She's tired,' she told him softly. 'We'd better go.'

Even Emma, still sobbing, didn't demur at that. Lacey put a hand on her shoulder and was startled when Emma squirmed away from it. Trying not to be hurt, she reminded herself that Emma *was* tired, and that all children had their unreasonable moments. Even adults did. Emma would get over this and be contrite, probably, by morning.

Emma climbed into the rear seat of the car and sniffed all the way home into the paper napkin she'd grabbed from the table. Lacey, torn between a desire to join her in the back and cuddle her and an almost equally strong desire to snap at her, sat tense and silent, and Tully still wore a faint scowl.

She was a little surprised but didn't object when he followed them inside. Emma bolted straight for the bathroom and closed the door. The cat, which had been waiting for them on the doorstep, wound itself around Lacey's legs, purring.

'Coffee?' Lacey suggested. They'd left the restaurant before having any.

'Yes,' Tully said on an exhaled breath. 'What brought that on? Was I too hard on her?'

Giving him an absent smile as she poured water into the jug, Lacey said, 'She's not accustomed to you growling at her.'

'She was way out of line. You don't allow her to talk to you like that, do you?'

'No. But I thought that you basically agreed with her. It isn't that I want to blight her life, you know.'

'Of course I know that!' he said impatiently. 'I do wonder, though, if you resent the fact that I can afford to give her things that are too expensive for your budget. Not that your budget needs to be so tight—'

'We've been through all that,' Lacey sighed. 'I told you, having you contribute towards Emma's keep is only fair, but anything more would make me feel like a kept woman.'

'A fate worse than death, obviously,' he said, sounding rather irritable. 'Okay, I know. We've covered that.'

'I don't resent you,' Lacey said, although she recalled times when she'd felt distinctly resentful of his freedom to come and go, of the small impact their mutual mistake had really made on his life as compared to hers. But she didn't honestly feel she'd allowed that to colour her attitude. 'And I don't resent your money.' At least that part was wholly true. 'But I can't allow Emma to think she can have everything she wants without any effort on her part. I don't want her to be like—'

She stopped, flushing.

'You don't want her to be like me,' Tully finished for her, his voice flat.

'I didn't mean that exactly,' she muttered.

'Something like it, then.' Tully paused. 'Sure I got every expensive toy I ever asked for. But my parents gave me things *instead* of their attention—their love. I give Emma things *out of* love.'

'Maybe that's so, but how is a child to know the difference?'

'She knows because she knows I love her. Just as I knew that *my* parents didn't give a damn.'

'I'm sure that's not true, of your mother at least. She cared enough to thoroughly dislike Francine.'

'Oh, in a mild fashion she was fond of me, as long as I didn't get in her way. But her dislike of Francine was a social thing rather than emotional. My mother, I'm afraid, is a snob.'

Lacey knew that. Mrs Cleaver had tolerated Francine as a holiday diversion for her son, but made it clear she wasn't going to have an ambitious little girl from a family of nobodies making any permanent claims on him. As Lacey recalled, after their very first meeting Francine had been in a flaming temper and had taken it out on Tully, who had seemed to regard the whole thing as rather funny.

The bathroom door opened and closed, and when Emma didn't appear in the kitchen Lacey said, 'She must be going straight to bed.'

'Sulking?'

'More likely ashamed of herself, I'd say, and embarrassed.'

'I'll give her a few minutes and then go and say goodnight, if that's okay?'

'Yes, of course.' If he felt bad about making her cry it was understandable that he wanted to talk to Emma again tonight. Lacey would go in to her later. 'She's been a bit quiet this week, I think,' she added thoughtfully. 'Was she okay with you?'

'I thought so, until this evening. Do you think something's bothering her?'

'Maybe. But she says not. Coffee's ready.'

They drank it in near-silence, neither feeling a need to talk. The thought occurred to Lacey that they'd shared many moments like this, but there would be fewer of them in future. Experiencing a tug of regret, she reminded herself that she'd also been desperately lonely at times, while Tully had always had a full social life. He would hardly miss sitting at a kitchen table occasionally with a woman who wasn't sharing his bed and had no intention of doing so.

He finished his drink first and got up, going down the passageway to Emma's room. He was back within the minute, saying ruefully, 'Left it too long, I guess. She's fast asleep.'

'Never mind, she won't hold it against you, I'm sure.'

Gathering up the empty cups, Lacey yawned, and Tully said, 'Is that a hint?'

'No, but it's been a fairly tiring day.'

'You should take it easy, after being sick.'

'So should you. You had it first.'

'I haven't spent the day digging.'

'Neither have I. A bit of weeding, that's all.'

'You don't think Emma's getting the bug?' he worried.

'Not now, surely? I did wonder earlier in the week.'

'I'll call in tomorrow on my way home from the office. Make sure she's okay.'

'You could eat with us if you like.'

Tully shook his head. 'Sorry, I've got something else on.'

She didn't think she'd shown any reaction, but he said rather edgily, 'It's a *meeting*. I can't get out of it.'

'You needn't,' she assured him hastily. 'I'm sure Emma will get over whatever it is.'

She rattled the cups into the sink and had her hands in soapy water when he briefly closed a hand on her shoulder and brushed her cheek with his lips and murmured, 'See you tomorrow.'

When he came he didn't stay long, and Emma, seeming to have forgotten her small tantrum, greeted him with unalloyed pleasure. Nothing was said about her behaviour the night before or her father's unprecedented rebuke, and by the time he left she'd extracted a promise to take her riding again on the following Saturday. Looking at her sparkling eyes as she skipped back into the house after waving him goodbye, Lacey decided that whatever had been affecting her, she must have got over it.

'Why don't you come with us?' Emma said. 'You'd like it, Mum.'

'Maybe one day I will.' She would wait for Tully to suggest it, though.

*   *   *

Having spent the previous Saturday alone, Lacey accepted Julian's suggestion of taking the chance to visit an exhibition of Pacific art at a city gallery.

'We could have dinner afterwards,' he said. 'Make an evening of it.'

'I think I should be home with Emma in the evening,' Lacey demurred. 'Why don't you have dinner with us?' After the briefest pause she added, 'Bring Desma if you like.'

'Good idea. Desma said she'd baby-sit again any time. So maybe we could go out after dinner.'

Lacey told Emma on Friday that Julian would be dining with them the following day. They were in the kitchen after school, Emma drinking a glass of milk while Lacey peeled potatoes for their meal. 'Is Desma coming, too?' she asked.

'Do you want her to come?'

Emma stared at her as if she'd sprouted horns. 'No,' she said baldly. 'I don't like her.'

Lacey kept her voice mild. 'You hardly know her. Isn't it a bit unfair to decide you don't like her?'

Emma looked quite fierce. 'It's not unfair. I can't help it. I don't want her here ever again!'

Lacey rinsed a potato, dried her hands, and sat down at the table opposite her daughter. The cat was curled up on another chair, and she idly stroked it as she asked quietly, 'Can you tell me why?'

Emma flushed. 'You don't care!' she said.

'Darling, you know I care very much about you.'

'Are you going to marry Julian?' Emma demanded.

This wasn't the way she'd meant to break the news. Lacey inwardly winced. 'I'm thinking about it,' she temporised. 'Emma, you needn't be worried that I'll ever stop loving you, or not love you as much.'

'I don't believe you!'

Shocked at the stark statement, Lacey was momentarily at a loss. Before she could frame a reply Emma burst out, 'If you really loved me you'd never have gone out with Julian and left me with *her*!'

'Emma!' She stretched out a hand, but Emma evaded it, jumping up from the table to flee to her room.

As the door slammed behind her Ruffles lifted his head, then settled down again, his tail curling more tightly about his pink nose. Lacey sat for a few moments, then went down the passageway and tapped on the door before letting herself in.

Emma lay on her bed facing the wall. She didn't move when Lacey sat down by her and laid a hand on her shoulder. 'Tell me all about it,' she said gently.

Emma's voice was muffled in the pillow. 'You won't listen!'

'I'm listening.'

'I hate Desma, and I hate Julian. I want it to be just us, you and me and Daddy, like before.'

Oh, dear. Jealousy. This required careful handling. 'Things can't always stay the same,' Lacey said. 'Sometimes change is good for people, like when Daddy bought us this house and we moved into it.'

No response.

'Emma, you know I love you more than anything in the world.'

Emma turned. 'Then tell Julian and Desma to go away. *Please*, Mummy!'

Her heart wrenched, Lacey said hesitantly, 'I can't do that without a reason.'

'I *told* you!' Emma cried, presenting her back again. 'I hate them! You don't really love me at *all*!'

In the end Lacey gave up. Troubled, she returned to the kitchen and mechanically tried to concentrate on cooking. She supposed it was natural for Emma to feel threatened, insecure. After all, she'd been the centre of Lacey's world all her life, and still was. It must be hard for a ten-year-old to understand that there was still room in her mother's heart for other kinds of love, other people.

But quite apart from the effect on Lacey and Julian, surely it wouldn't be good for a child to find she could smash her mother's relationship with a perfectly nice man, on a whim?

Later Emma emerged and set the table, but all evening she was subdued, evading Lacey's eyes. After her bath, when Lacey went into her bedroom to say goodnight, she was either asleep or pretending to be, with Ruffles settled down beside her.

Lacey phoned Julian. After hearing her out, he said, 'I wouldn't worry about it. She'll come round.'

'I hope so. I want her to be happy about it.'

'Emma's young. She'll just have to get used to the idea.'

'*Have* to?' She hadn't meant to sound sharp, but that was how it came out.

'We can't let the immature prejudice of a ten-year-old spoil our future together, Lacey.'

She'd been telling herself much the same thing, but somehow hearing him say it made her hackles rise.

'Can we?' Julian asked reasonably, into the silence.

'No,' she said, 'of course not. But she needs some time to get used to the idea.'

Just before Tully was due to pick Emma up on Saturday, she turned to her mother and asked, 'Are you still going out with Julian today?'

'Yes,' Lacey said truthfully. 'I've promised. We're going to see some paintings. By the way,' she added, 'Desma will be here for dinner, too.'

Emma's eyes flickered, her soft mouth acquiring a stubborn look that Lacey knew all too well. But all she said was, 'Will Daddy be staying too?'

'Oh, I expect your father has other things to do tonight,' Lacey guessed. 'You'll be with him all the afternoon.'

'*You're* not going out, are you? At night?'

Lacey said carefully, 'We did hope to go out in the evening, if you and Desma don't mind.' Emma's eyes had gone enormous suddenly, and Lacey paused. 'But if you don't want—'

Emma wasn't listening. She had darted past her mother and down the passageway to wrench open the door. '*Daddy*!'

Tully was on the step, and Emma flung herself at him, winding her arms tightly about him. She must have heard the car while Lacey was preoccupied in talking to her.

'Hi,' he said, ruffling her hair with one big hand. 'Ready to go?'

'Yes,' Emma said, her face hidden against his jacket. 'I want to go now!'

'Well, say goodbye to your mother.'

Emma shook her head without moving it away.

Tully raised his brows at Lacey, now standing in the doorway and watching Emma with a puzzled frown. 'Trouble?' he mouthed.

'I'll get her jacket,' Lacey said. Maybe Emma would come round in the course of the afternoon. It was no use trying to argue the matter out now. She collected the jacket and handed it to Tully, who was lounging in the doorway. Emma, she saw, was already ensconced in the passenger seat of the car.

'Did you have a row?' he asked.

'Not exactly. I've invited Julian and Desma for dinner and she isn't happy about it. For some reason she's taken an unreasonable dislike to Desma.'

'Unreasonable?'

Lacey sighed. 'Desma's a perfectly nice girl.'

'Is she?' He sounded sceptical.

'*Yes*,' Lacey said firmly. 'Here, take Emma's jacket and enjoy your day.' She and Emma hardly ever rowed, and she hated having Tully walk into the middle of it. And she was worried by the look on Emma's face just before he'd arrived.

Julian and Desma were both in the lounge and Lacey had left them for a few minutes to check on the casserole, when the kitchen door opened and Tully and Emma entered hand in hand. They were later than usual, and Lacey had begun to be anxious.

Emma looked pale, her eyes slightly pink-rimmed, and Tully's face was grim.

Lacey's heart contracted with fright. 'What happened?' she asked. 'Did you have an accident?'

'No accident.' Tully looked at her with a strangely hostile glare. 'I'm sorry we're late.'

She waited for an explanation, but apparently none was going to come. She looked at Emma again. 'Emma, what's wrong?'

'Nothing.' Emma looked away from her and then back again, her gaze almost defiant. 'Can Daddy stay for tea?'

Lacey cast a quick look at the dark, silent man, waiting for him to make some polite excuse. He knew she was entertaining Julian tonight.

He stared back at her, his expression very much like his daughter's, his eyes nearly black, fierce and demanding.

She said, 'We have other guests tonight, Emma.'

Emma's face went stubborn, making her look more like her father than ever. 'I want Daddy, too.'

Why didn't Tully say something? If Lacey refused point blank it would alienate Emma further from Julian, she knew. 'Well, all right,' she said finally. Her eyes searched her daughter's. Had Emma been crying or was the pinkness the result of the fresh, cold breeze outside? 'Why don't you go and take off your jacket?'

When the child had finally let go of Tully's hand and left the room, Lacey turned and asked Tully, 'What's going on?'

He was shrugging out of his jacket. 'Emma wants me to stay,' he said curtly. And with a hint of irony, 'Thanks for the invitation.'

'You know perfectly well I was forced into inviting you,' she snapped.

'And maybe I was forced into accepting,' he countered.

'Emma doesn't have to have everything she wants.'

'She needs some moral support.'

'Tully—she can't be allowed to manipulate adults just to get her own way.'

He looked blazingly angry suddenly. 'So what about adults manipulating a child? Is that supposed to be all right?'

'I'm not!' she protested. 'All I want is to give her a chance to get to know Julian and Desma.'

'Emma said you and Julian were going out?'

'That was the original plan, but if Emma's not happy about it—'

'She's not.'

'Ah!' Julian had appeared in the doorway, a glass in his hand. 'I thought I heard voices. Hello, Tully. Lacey was getting worried about Emma.'

Tully nodded to him. 'We were held up.'

Still no explanation, Lacey noted with exasperation. 'Tully's staying for dinner,' she said shortly, 'as it's so late.'

Tully threw her a quizzical glance.

Julian said quite amiably, 'Oh, really? Well, come and meet my daughter.'

'Yes,' Tully said, smiling. 'I certainly want to meet Desma.'

Lacey looked at that smile and alarm bells started ringing in her mind. But when she said, 'Tully...' he turned a perfectly bland, enquiring face to her.

'Never mind,' she muttered, trying to signal him with her eyes, Whatever you're planning, *don't*!

The two men went into the other room, and Lacey turned to take the casserole out of the oven, burning her hand in the process. Just as well what she'd decided on for a main dish would stretch, although the prime consideration had been to cook a meal that wouldn't entail a lot of preparation between arriving home and serving it.

Desma had politely offered to help, but it was mainly just a matter of heating things and setting the table, a task Desma had accomplished quickly and neatly before Lacey had suggested the three of them should have drinks in the lounge while waiting for Emma.

As she ran cold water on her smarting hand she heard Desma's voice and Tully's deep one, and Julian's, lighter and less audible but ending in a laugh. That should have reassured her but somehow it didn't.

She hurried through the rest of the preparations and called them all into the dining room, relieved to see that Emma had joined them and was sitting on the arm of her father's chair, his arm loosely about her waist.

Over dinner she watched, dismayed and perplexed, as Tully deliberately charmed Desma, gently teasing her like a favourite uncle. The girl sat with flushed cheeks and sparkling eyes and gave pert, giggling answers to his smiling questions. She didn't seem to notice that when the smile faded his eyes were quietly calculating.

Emma, seated next to her father, was almost silent, and Julian was determined to keep Lacey's attention on himself. She suspected he was compensating for Tully's presence.

When the meal was over Tully looked at them and said lazily, 'You two wanted to go out, didn't you?'

'We haven't decided,' Lacey said quickly.

'It's okay. Daddy said he'd stay with me,' Emma cut in, casting Tully a look of adoring gratitude.

Desma said, 'Oh, I'm baby-sitting. I don't have anything else to do.'

'What, a pretty girl like you,' Tully said, 'with nothing
better to do on a Saturday night? Don't you have a boyfriend or something?'

'Not just now.'

'Plenty of time for that,' Julian said. 'Thanks for the
offer, Tully. And if you're going to be here, Desma can
come with us.'

Lacey noticed that Emma had hold of Tully's arm,
but now the small hand dropped to her lap.

'It's all right, honestly,' Desma was saying brightly.
'We'll be okay, won't we, Emma?'

It was the first time she had directly addressed Emma
all evening, though admittedly Tully had tended to mon-
opolise her attention. Her eyes were fixed on the younger
girl. 'Won't we?' she repeated.

Tully moved with apparent casualness, his arm resting
on the back of Emma's chair, his hand lightly on her
shoulder. 'That's very kind of you, Desma,' he said
pleasantly, 'but you see, I promised Emma I'd stay, as
her mother's going out.'

'But Dad told me—' Desma turned to Julian, the rising
note in her voice making Lacey glance sharply at her.
She looked thoroughly put out.

Julian said, 'Yes...but we have a change of plan.
Where would you two ladies like to go?'

Desma said, 'I'm not coming!'

Lacey, victim of a growing unease, felt like making
the same statement. After all, she hadn't exactly
promised Julian they could go anywhere. On the other
hand, if Tully was willing to mind Emma there was no
reason to stay in, was there? 'Perhaps—' she began tentatively, but no one was taking any notice of her.

Julian was saying, 'If Tully's going to be here, Desma,
there's no need for you to stay.'

'You two don't want me along,' Desma objected.

'Nonsense!' her father said. 'We don't mind, do we, Lacey?'

'No, of course not,' Lacey agreed hastily, 'but we don't really have to go anywh—'

Tully interrupted. 'Desma doesn't want to play gooseberry, do you?' He turned a high-wattage smile on her. 'If you want to stay here, it's okay with us, isn't it, Emma?'

Emma looked up at him, a tiny crease marring her smooth childish brow before she nodded obediently.

'So the choice is yours,' Tully told Desma easily.

Julian cleared his throat. 'I'd prefer Desma to come with us.'

A slight irritation put a snap in Lacey's voice. 'There's really no need for anyone to go anywhere.' Hadn't Julian said he wanted the girls to get to know each other? Now they had a chance to spend some time together, with Tully to act as buffer, and Julian seemed determined to spoil it.

'Now, there's an idea,' Tully said, laughter in his voice. 'We could all stay in and play Scrabble or. . .'

'Or Happy Families, no doubt!' Lacey said, just as he added, '. . . something.'

He looked at her across the table and laughed outright. His voice dripping with kindness, he said, 'You need a night out, Lacey. Don't you think so, Julian?'

'I'm glad you agree,' Julian said heartily.

'And I promise I'll take good care of both girls.'

Julian looked doubtfully from him to Desma. 'The thing is. . .'

Tully's face, his whole manner, suddenly changed. 'Julian,' he said quietly, and waited for the other man to meet his eyes. 'Your daughter is in no danger from me.'

Julian flushed. 'I'm sorry—'

'Don't be,' Tully returned swiftly. 'I have a little girl, too.'

Appalled, Lacey said, 'Tully wouldn't—'

Tully flashed her a smile. 'Thanks, but Julian doesn't know me as well as you do.' He turned to Desma and said gently, 'You'd better go with your father and Lacey.'

Lacey was surprised at the look of near-panic that flashed across the girl's face. 'No, I want to stay. Dad— I'm not a child!'

But she was no match for both her father and Tully. When they left the house Lacey was already exhausted and Desma was sulking, despite the fact that Tully had invited her to help him with the dishes while Emma prepared for bed and Lacey freshened herself up.

Julian suggested a film, and drove them into the city. They were about to enter the theatre when Desma said, 'Dad, have you got some coins? Cathy asked me to phone her and tell her what our English homework is for the weekend. She missed the last period on Friday.'

'Can't you do it tomorrow?' Julian had the tickets in his hand. 'The film starts in a few minutes.'

'I won't be long. She might want to do it tonight. There's a phone booth just over there.'

'Well, make it quick, then. Kids!' Julian muttered to Lacey as Desma hurried over to the box.

Lacey smiled, idly watching as the girl stopped, looked at the booth and swung round to return to them. 'It only takes cards!' she said.

Julian shrugged. 'It'll have to wait until tomorrow.'

'But it's *urgent*!'

Irritably, Julian asked, 'If it's so important why didn't you remember before?'

'I did! I tried to phone from Lacey's but it was engaged.'

That was news to Lacey, not that she minded. 'I might have a card,' she said, fishing in her small bag, but the hopeful look in Desma's anxious eyes died when she said, 'No, sorry. It must be in my other bag.'

'Come on,' Julian said. 'We've wasted enough time.'

Desma reluctantly trailed after him, and spent most of the film fidgeting in her seat and chewing on a thumbnail. Lacey didn't think any of them enjoyed their evening out much, and when Julian half-heartedly suggested supper afterwards they both turned it down. Lacey just wanted to go home, and she had the distinct feeling that Desma felt the same way.

She almost expected Julian to just drop her off and leave, but his manners were too good for that. When she invited them in he said, 'We won't stay long, but I should just say thanks to Tully for giving us the time together.'

She led the way into the lounge where Tully was sitting in one of the fireside chairs. A young man in narrow jeans and a leather jacket sat opposite, a sullen expression on his face.

Lacey heard Desma give a choking gasp as Tully rose to his feet, apparently jerking the boy up with a look and a sharp movement of his head, as though he were invisibly wired.

Julian came to Lacey's side, saying in thunderstruck tones, 'What the hell is he doing here?'

And Tully, his eyes not moving from the stranger, said, 'Lacey, this is Bryce. He's been a visitor here before... haven't you, Bryce?'

CHAPTER SEVEN

'I DON'T think...' Lacey began uncertainly, only to be interrupted by Julian.

'*He's what*?'

Tully said, 'He came looking for Desma tonight. I explained that she'd gone out with you two, and persuaded him to wait. We've had quite a chat.'

The young man looked hunted, his eyes sliding past Tully's. He swallowed, his Adam's apple moving convulsively.

Julian said, 'Desma?' He found her standing near the doorway as if contemplating backing through it. 'What's been going on? You told me you weren't seeing Bryce any more.'

Bryce seemed to find his voice. 'Yeah, she told you that to stop you going on at her all the time.'

'*Desma*?' Julian said again.

Desma looked at her father sulkily. 'We did break up but we got back together again. And I know you don't like Bryce, so we decided...' she shrugged '...*I* decided,' she amended, 'not to tell you. It just saved a lot of hassle.'

'You've been seeing this boy behind my back?'

'I didn't want you nagging me all the time, like before.'

Tully said, 'Perhaps you two can sort that out later. The point is, Desma invited Bryce round here last time she was baby-sitting, didn't you, Desma?'

The girl's eyes darted to Bryce, then to her father, and were unwillingly dragged back to Tully's face, stern and with no hint of the laughter that had charmed her earlier. 'What if I did?'

106

'And you repeated the invitation for tonight.'

She looked away again. 'We weren't *doing* anything,' she muttered. 'It was just a place to be alone, that's all.'

'But you didn't want your dad to know about it.'

Desma silently shook her head.

'And you let Bryce in when you thought Emma had gone to sleep.'

'She *was* asleep! Well, she looked asleep. I s'pose she might have been pretending.'

Lacey's mouth had dried. 'Tully, what's this all about?' she demanded.

Julian said, 'Look, I'm sorry about this, Lacey. You had no right, Desma, to invite anyone into Lacey's home without her permission. I'm very disappointed in you. We'd better go home and have a good talk.'

He made to take his daughter's arm, but Tully's voice stopped him. 'Not yet!'

Julian turned. 'This is between my daughter and me—'

'It involves *my* daughter,' Tully said. 'Tell us what happened, Desma. The night you were supposedly caring for Emma.'

Desma looked at Bryce. 'Nothing,' she said unconvincingly.

Bryce said, 'I told you—'

'*Shut up!*' Lacey blinked at the savagery in Tully's voice. 'I'm asking Desma now.'

'It was nothing, honestly,' the girl said in a frightened voice.

Even Julian obviously didn't believe her. He looked uncertain, and deeply anxious.

Miraculously, Tully's manner changed, became almost coaxing. 'Something happened,' he contradicted her. 'I need you to tell us, Desma.' He paused. 'Emma woke up, didn't she? Just when you and Bryce had settled down for a cosy evening together.'

Desma bit her lip, glanced again at Bryce and, receiving no help, nodded. 'She went to let the cat in.'

'And she saw you and Bryce in the lounge.'

'We were listening to music!' Desma said. 'I suppose that's why I didn't hear the cat. There's nothing wrong with that, is there?'

Tully smiled at her, his voice soothing. 'I'm sure you weren't doing anything wrong.' Did she notice that his eyes held no warmth? 'You just didn't want your father to know you'd invited Bryce around here. So what did you do?'

Lacey's breath caught, her skin going cold. What was Tully getting at?

'I didn't do anything,' Desma said sulkily. 'I never touched her!' she said more loudly. 'And Bryce didn't, either.'

Her eyes on the young man's face, Lacey heard herself speak, the words torn from her throat, terror thickening her voice. '*What did you do to Emma?*'

'Like she said, I never touched the kid!' He looked quite scared, himself.

Lacey felt sick. Emma, who chattered constantly about everything she did, everything she saw, had never mentioned seeing anyone with Desma that night. She'd been so quiet afterwards Lacey had thought she was coming down with something. '*What did you do?*' she reiterated, so fiercely that as she took a step towards him the boy shrank back. 'You threatened her, didn't you?'

Bryce, finding himself closer to Tully, looked from him to Lacey and blustered, 'I don't have to talk to you! You're not the cops.'

Tully said immediately, 'If you'd rather talk to them, it can easily be arranged.'

Desma said, 'Oh, tell them, Bryce! They can't put you in jail for *talking* to someone, can they?'

Bryce scowled at her.

'He talked to Emma, then?' Tully said. 'What did he say, Desma?'

'I...I didn't hear all of it.'

Lacey's throat locked. 'You left her alone with him?'

'No! Not really.'

'What—' Lacey started.

But Tully cut across her. 'What does that mean, Desma?'

'I don't know what you're getting all uptight about.' Desma glanced defiantly at Lacey. 'She...Emma asked a lot of questions, and I told her it was none of her business and to go back to bed. She took the cat with her, and Bryce said...he said we'd better talk to her, make her promise not to tell.'

'*Make* her...?' Lacey repeated, her hands clenching.

'Let Desma finish,' Tully said quietly.

Lacey cast him a resentful look, but his eyes were on Desma. 'Go on,' he said.

She shrugged. 'Well...he just sat down on the bed and talked to her, and...I stayed in the doorway. He didn't *hurt* her! He didn't even *say* he would. And he wouldn't *really* have—'

In the abrupt silence Lacey could hear someone walking along the street outside, and the sound of a distant siren fading away.

'What wouldn't he really do?' Tully asked softly.

Desma looked helplessly at Bryce. 'You didn't mean it,' she said weakly, 'did you?'

'*What*?' Tully turned to Bryce. 'Come on, spit it out.'

'Ask her,' the boy sneered, jerking his head in Desma's direction. 'Silly bitch can't keep her mouth shut, anyway. Just like a woman.'

Desma's eyes widened, her face going pale. But Bryce wasn't looking at her. He was uneasily eyeing Tully.

Without moving, Tully said evenly, 'I'm asking you. And you're going to tell me, Bryce. What did you say you would do if Emma told?'

The boy hunched his shoulders inside his jacket, his hands jammed into the pockets. 'Kill her f . . . her effin' cat,' he said, and forced a snickering laugh. 'Nah, I didn't mean it. I just wanted to shut her up, that's all. I didn't even have a knife on me. Jeeze—all this fuss 'cause a stupid kid got a bit of a fright—'

'Get out.'

Bryce stopped in mid-flow, looked at Tully, gulped once and then made for the door at a near-run, brushing past Julian and not even looking at Desma.

The front door slammed behind him. Desma was crying, Lacey realised, tears rolling down her cheeks.

Lacey was shaking, herself. She wanted to go and check on Emma, make sure she was all right. And she didn't want to be in the same room with Desma. Well, Desma was Julian's daughter, let him deal with it. 'Maybe you'd better take her home, now,' she suggested to him, her lips feeling oddly stiff.

'Yes,' he said. 'I'm deeply sorry, Lacey. She's been incredibly foolish, but fortunately no real harm has been done.'

Lacey stared at him, wanting to scream at him, *What do you mean, no real harm . . .*? Emma had been terrorised in her own home, her own bed, by some unknown young thug, had been worrying for days that her beloved pet would be in danger if she told her mother what had happened, been too scared to give the real reason why she didn't want to be left in Desma's charge again, and worst of all, Lacey had let her down badly, putting it all down to simple jealousy!

'Desma,' Julian said, 'you owe Lacey an apology.'

Desma sniffed, and Lacey said, 'Not now, Julian! Take her home, please.' She really didn't want to look at Desma right now. She was afraid that if they stayed here one minute longer she'd end up flying at the girl, giving in to an urge to slap her. Lacey didn't believe in physical violence, but she kept thinking of Emma as she had looked just before Tully arrived today. Oh, *why* hadn't she realised that something was desperately wrong?

'Yes,' Julian said heavily. 'I'll phone you.' He put a hand on Desma's heaving shoulder and said, 'Come on then, we'll talk about this at home.'

Even before the outer door closed behind them, Lacey went flying down the passageway to Emma's room. The door was ajar and she stopped herself, calming her breathing before pushing it open and tiptoeing inside.

Emma was curled on her side with Ruffles nestled in the curve of her body. The cat's ear twitched, and one gleaming feline eye opened and closed again. Emma's breathing was regular, and a trail of dark hair lay across her cheek.

Lacey smoothed it gently back and bent to kiss the warm skin. 'Emma, darling! I'm so sorry!' she whispered. Tomorrow she'd say it again, when Emma was awake to hear it. Her heart contracted. How could anyone do that to a defenceless child? Anger and guilt made her hand unsteady as she adjusted the covers before creeping out of the room.

Tully stood waiting for her a few feet away.

'She's all right,' Lacey said unnecessarily.

'I know.' He followed her back to the lighted lounge. 'Do you want a drink?'

Lacey shook her head. She supposed she was looking as though she needed one, but that wasn't important. 'Did Emma tell you?' she asked him.

'Not really. I knew something was wrong, she admitted that much, but she said she'd sworn not to tell. But she let slip enough for me to guess that Desma hadn't been alone last time she baby-sat. And today Emma was obviously petrified that you were going to go out with Julian again tonight and leave her with Desma.'

She wouldn't have, of course. Not if Emma was that frightened . . . and yet Emma had been scared ever since the last time, and somehow Lacey had failed to recognise it. She wasn't sure if she would ever forgive herself for that.

'In future,' Tully said, 'I'll stay with Emma when you're out with Julian.'

'There's no need for that. I can get Mrs Dillon or the girl across the road. Emma's used to them both.'

'I promised her.'

'But, Tully—'

'I promised Emma,' he reiterated, 'and you were the one who said I mustn't break a promise to her. So next time you and Julian have plans, contact me.'

'Suppose you have plans of your own?'

'I'll change them.'

He looked grimly determined and she stopped arguing. Maybe Emma did need him for a while. 'How did you know Desma was expecting Bryce tonight?' she asked him.

'I didn't know, I just had a hunch that they might try it again. And the way she reacted when I said I'd stay with Emma, I knew I was right.'

Inwardly Lacey winced. He'd picked up all the clues; why hadn't she? 'I thought you liked her,' she said.

'I wanted to wring her deceitful little neck,' Tully confessed. 'But you catch more flies with honey than vinegar. I kind of hoped that I'd get her to talk to me if you and Julian left us alone. Only your boyfriend apparently had me pegged as a cradle snatcher—'

'That's not fair! Julian was just being a sensible parent.'

Tully nodded. 'Okay,' he conceded. 'I guess. I did,' he admitted, 'understand his concern. So I figured I'd just wait and let the guy in if he arrived. I was afraid she might manage to contact him and warn him off, though.'

'When we got to the theatre she tried to call someone, but we had no phone cards. She said it was a school friend she wanted to get hold of.'

'She told me the same story when she used the dining room phone here. I stayed around in the doorway, and she said the number was engaged.'

'He must have got a shock to find you here.'

'You could say that. I think he would have spilled the beans in another minute if you hadn't come in. I had him very nervous.'

'I noticed.' Lacey remembered how formidable he'd looked, how his voice had commanded, threatened. 'I didn't know you could be so...aggressive.'

'Only when it's necessary.'

She looked at him, and he said, 'What's the matter? Did I scare you?'

She shook her head. If he'd been scary it was on Emma's behalf. 'You love Emma very much, don't you?'

'I guess I do.'

Feeling her way, she said, 'Desma's only a kid herself. You won't...you wouldn't hold it against Julian, would you?'

His face closed, became a still, cold mask. 'If you're asking me again to endorse your marriage, forget it.'

'I'm sorry you feel that way.' Lacey squared her shoulders. 'I'm not going to back out be-cause...because I made a mistake in trusting Desma.'

'Has it occurred to you that you're making a much bigger mistake than that?'

'What do you mean?'

'What the hell do you think I mean?' He sounded exasperated. 'Julian, of course. Do you really think you can be happy with him?'

'He's a very nice man.'

'Sure,' Tully agreed. 'Is that what you want?'

'I certainly don't see anything wrong with it,' Lacey said, adding firmly, '*Julian* is what I want.'

'Really.' He sounded totally scornful.

'Yes, really!' Lacey flared.

'Do you know what?' he said, as if he'd just discovered something. 'I don't believe you.'

'Well, you'll just have to take my word for it,' Lacey said.

'Yeah?' He seemed poised, as though debating a well-planned move. 'I don't know about that.'

She looked at him suspiciously, experiencing a sudden surge of adrenalin, an instinctive urge to flee. But instead she stood her ground. 'What are you getting at, Tully?'

His lips curled in a strangely predatory smile, and he came towards her. She tried to take a step backwards, but he'd already snared her waist with his arm, hardly exerting himself at all to bring her snugly against him, his other hand caressing her nape. 'I need proof,' he said, and as she opened her mouth to say *Don't*! he covered it with his, in a kiss of frank, uninhibited passion that allowed her no room for escape.

She tried to fight it at first, closed her fists and pushed, then pounded, at his arms and shoulders. She lifted a foot to stamp on his, and he moved swiftly without releasing her mouth, shifted his feet and clamped her thigh between his, so that she involuntarily drew a quick, shuddering breath and let it out again, breathing into his open mouth. She sank her hands into his hair, twisted her fingers into it, and felt the answering, warning tug of his fingers in her own hair. Pausing, she was conscious of the silky strands between her fingers, and a treacherous memory rose in her mind, suffused her body, heated her blood.

His mouth moved compellingly on hers, his teeth gently nipping at her lower lip, and now she was off balance, curved intimately into his embrace, her heart pounding as he cradled her head against the curve of his shoulder and ran his hand knowingly down her back, then up over her rib cage to find her breast.

That was when she stopped resisting, stopped trying to fight it, and let her hands stroke through his hair as they wanted to, her body press itself closer to him, her mouth accept the hungry, seeking thrust of his tongue. The kiss seemed to last forever, and when at last he allowed some space between them he looked at her with his eyes brilliant and dark and said, 'Now tell me it's Julian you want.'

Dazed, she stared back at him, trying to bring the world back into perspective. He was smiling at her, the smile of a conqueror, a man who knew he was invincible. And his hands were on the front of her dress, quietly, deliberately undoing the buttons of her shirt-waister.

She put her own hands up and tangled her fingers in his. Belatedly she managed the one word that she should have said minutes ago. 'Don't.'

It came out hoarse and barely audible, but he stopped what he was doing and repeated, *'Don't?'* He was still smiling, confident. He gathered her hands into his and swept them aside, parting the two halves of her bodice as well, exposing a satin and lace bra that barely covered the generous curves of her breasts. 'Mmm,' he said, as though he'd spied a particularly delicious dessert. His head bent, and he whipped her hands behind her, bending her backwards as he nuzzled the rounded softness, his cheek rasping a little on her skin, his mouth warm and moist.

Lacey shivered with pleasure and clenched her teeth. 'Tully, stop!'

Reluctantly he lifted his head, and looked into her flushed face. 'Why?' he enquired in soft, pained tones. 'It was just getting interesting.'

It was just getting damned dangerous, Lacey thought wildly. 'Let me go, Tully,' she said, her voice shaking.

For a moment his face wore that stubborn, immovable look that Emma had inherited. Then he sighed and straightened, letting his hands drop, but his eyes lingered on her breasts until she pulled her dress across them with unsteady fingers. Then his gaze drifted up to meet hers. 'Off limits?' he said regretfully, a spark of laughter in his eyes.

'Most definitely off limits, to you!' She tried to sound dignified and very, very positive.

'It was nice, though, wasn't it?' he said, a smile curving his mouth, his eyes, still holding a hot glaze of desire, lingering regretfully over her.

She felt her body's unthinking reaction and snapped, 'Damn it, Tully! You have no *right*—'

'Don't I?' he countered, as if there could be any argument about it. 'Do you have the right to marry Julian when you respond like that to me?'

'That has nothing to do with anything!' As his brows rose in amused scepticism, she went on recklessly, 'A simple biological reflex, that's all, because it's been so long since—'

By the time she stopped herself it was far too late. Tully looked at first stunned, and then his expression became one of unholy fascination. 'Since what?' he taunted softly.

'Never mind!'

It was no use, of course. 'Since you made love with someone?' he enquired.

Of course she wasn't going to answer that and he knew it. But her silence didn't stop him. His lips curved in a diabolical smile that made her long to hit him. He said, 'You're not sleeping with Julian. What's the matter with the guy?'

'Nothing is the *matter* with him! Not every man is a tom-cat like...like some people.'

The smile faded, and the gleam in his eyes subtly altered. 'Like me.'

'If the cap fits...' She shrugged defiantly.

His mouth was very firm now. 'I don't know where you got that idea.'

'It isn't difficult to work out. I've known you for ten years.'

'And for ten years I've scrupulously kept my hands off you.' He must have seen the flicker of her eyelids, the slight flush that rose to her cheeks. 'Except once,' he conceded. 'All right, twice,' he amended as she gave him a withering look.

'Am I supposed to congratulate you? I don't suppose it was hard. There've been plenty of other women in your life in that time.'

'Some,' he admitted curtly. 'What else did you expect?'

'I don't expect anything of you, Tully. I never have.' A man like Tully wouldn't have remained celibate, she knew that. It would never have occurred to her to ask it of him, and anyway, she'd never had the right.

'You think I've been sleeping around all these years, don't you?' he said accusingly.

'It's really none of my business. You're a free agent.'

For some reason that seemed to anger rather than placate him. His brows drew together and he looked as if he wanted to do something violent. Perhaps in order to stop himself, he swung away from her. 'Maybe your whole trouble is that you don't expect enough of people,' he said strangely, making rapidly for the door.

He paused there and looked around, giving her a peculiarly thorough look. His eyes still held a glittery fire. 'Yes,' he said almost to himself, 'things are going to change.'

She was still trying to work that out when she heard the door close decisively behind him.

She talked with Emma in the morning, told her that she knew all about what had happened, and that there was no chance of a repetition. 'But if anything like that happens again, tell me. And remember, a promise made because someone has frightened you doesn't have to be kept.'

'You won't leave me with Desma, ever?' Emma queried fearfully.

'I won't,' Lacey told her. 'But I'm sure Desma's truly sorry.'

'Daddy won't let that man kill Ruffles, will he?' Emma hugged the cat to her.

'Nobody will let that happen.'

Julian came round later in the day without Desma. 'She's quite ashamed of herself,' he said. 'I read the riot act last night, so you can be sure nothing like that will happen again. And she asked me to apologise.'

They were sitting at the kitchen table, and Julian reached over to place a hand on hers. 'I know you won't let it make any difference to us,' he said. 'You understand how difficult it is, bringing up children.'

'Yes, I understand,' Lacey said, 'and I don't blame you for what happened, Julian. But...'

Julian's hand tightened, squeezing hers. 'It'll be okay,' he said. 'We should have another family outing, the four of us.'

'No.' Her refusal was instant and unthinking, and she tried to temper it. 'Not yet. Emma needs time to get over this.'

'I think we ought to get the girls together as much as possible. Desma's a gentle girl, that's why that damned boy was able to dominate her. I want you and Emma to get to know her.'

Lacey had wanted it too, not so long ago. Now she wasn't so sure. 'I don't want to force Emma. Let's just leave it for a little while.'

A hint of impatience crossed his face. 'Don't you think it might be wiser not to pander too much to what Emma wants? She wasn't hurt.'

'Her trust in people is damaged. Her trust in me—' Lacey swallowed.

'All parents make mistakes,' he told her, and came round the table to place a hand on her shoulder. 'If anyone's to blame it's me, for suggesting Desma baby-sit.'

'No, you had the best of motives. But you understand that I can't leave Emma with her again.'

'Well, we'll leave that for the future,' Julian said vaguely. 'I do realise it won't happen again soon.'

Never! Lacey thought, biting her tongue. She didn't want to start an argument now.

Emma came back from her next riding lesson flushed with excitement. 'My instructor said I could go into a class and have group lessons with other kids every week. Daddy said I have to ask you, but he'll pay for them. It will be all right, won't it, Mum? She said lots of kids come out from town, but some of them are from round there, and they have their own horses. There's a pony club, too. I wish we could live there, but I can have the lessons, can't I?'

She did seem serious about riding, Lacey had to admit. 'I don't see why not,' she said, 'if your father is willing to take you out for them.'

'Will you come and watch? You could have a lesson too, if you like.'

The riding school was at Wiri, an area of rolling farmland where oddments of dark bush were tucked into the folds. Once entirely occupied by working dairy farms, the district was now also a haven for people who worked in the city but preferred a country lifestyle in their leisure time. Horses and cattle grazed on the neatly fenced green paddocks of small hobby farms, many of them boasting quite palatial homes.

'Your daughter,' the riding instructor told Lacey, 'has the makings of a good little rider. A bit over-confident, maybe.'

'Not like me, then,' Lacey said ruefully. 'She takes after her father.'

Tully cast her a quick look but said nothing. Today he elected to join her watching Emma's lesson rather than taking one himself. 'I know enough now to stay in the saddle and treat the horse right,' he told them. 'It's enough for me. Emma has her sights set on bigger things.'

Lush spring grass, emerald green and sweet-smelling, muffled the sound of the horses' hooves; lazy clouds drifted in a blue sky, and somewhere a lark was singing, clear and high. Hanging over the wooden fence watching her, with Tully by her side, Lacey felt a sudden dizzy zest in the day.

When they got back to the house the phone was ringing, and Lacey hurried into the dining room-cum-office to answer it.

'Lacey!' Julian sounded put out. 'I've been phoning you all day.'

'We've been out,' she explained.

'You and Emma?'

'And Tully,' she said, after the barest pause.

'I see. I thought we had an arrangement.' His voice was distinctly cold now.

'I'm sorry,' she said blankly. 'I don't recall that we arranged anything for today.'

'Not specifically,' he acknowledged. 'But you know we usually get together when Tully has Emma. We are engaged!'

Did that mean they had to spend every free moment with each other? 'I'm sorry,' she said again. 'I feel Emma needs some extra time right now.'

'You mean you feel guilty. Lacey, it wasn't your fault. Look, it's not too late. What about coming over here for dinner? Bring Emma.'

'That's a nice thought,' she said. It *was* a nice thought. But her heart sank at the thought of Emma's probable reaction. 'Just a second.'

Tully had put the kettle on and Emma was investigating the biscuit tin in the kitchen. 'Emma,' Lacey said in a determinedly cheerful voice, 'we've been invited to have dinner at Julian's place.'

Emma's small face froze. Tully's looked very similar, but much more forbidding.

Ignoring him, Lacey spoke gently to Emma. 'Julian and Desma feel bad about what happened. They want to make it up to you. I'll be there too.'

Emma swallowed. 'Can Daddy come?'

'Not this time. Daddy hasn't been invited.'

'We don't have to go, do we, Mummy? I want to stay home.'

Tully put a hand on Emma's shoulder. 'I'll stay here with Emma.'

Emma's face was a picture of relief and delight. 'Will you, Daddy? Thank you!'

'Go on,' Tully said, as Lacey hesitated. 'Tell him you'll be there.'

'Don't you have other things to do tonight?'

'No.' Tully looked down at Emma. 'Nothing I'd rather be doing. What shall we have for dinner, Em?'

'Can we have takeaways? And there's a programme about cats on TV tonight. We could watch that and then play Scrabble.'

For a moment Lacey felt shut out as Emma smiled back at Tully, obviously looking forward to spending the evening alone with him. Slowly she picked up the receiver again and said, 'Tully's going to look after Emma. I'll be coming on my own.'

Desma greeted Lacey offhandedly, and then disappeared to her room while her father gave Lacey a glass of wine and returned to cooking dinner.

'Desma's going out,' he said. 'I'd hoped to persuade her to stay in tonight,' he said, 'but as Emma isn't coming I suppose there's no real point.'

When she came out of her room Desma smelled like a perfume factory and was wearing a skin-tight, very short skirt with a cropped top. Julian looked at her askance. 'I thought you were going ice-skating?'

'We are.' She stared back at him. 'Can I have some money?'

Julian sighed and dug in his pocket, handing her a couple of notes. 'Here. Now, you're sure you don't need me to pick you up afterwards?'

'I told you, Sandy's mother's bringing me home. Well, enjoy yourselves, you two,' she added. 'Don't do anything I wouldn't do. Or if you do, do it *safely*!'

As she sashayed out the door Julian looked ruefully at Lacey. 'Kids.'

She gave him a perfunctory smile back and put down her wine. 'Can I help with anything?'

'You just relax. Dinner will be ready in about ten minutes.'

After dinner accompanied by another glass of wine, Julian insisted they didn't wash up, but instead steered her into the sitting room and towards the sofa. Settling himself beside her, he said, 'We seem to have had precious little time on our own lately.'

When he turned her to him and began kissing her, Lacey made a conscious effort to relax, but she found her mind wandering.

When Julian lifted his mouth from hers she said, 'Have you ever thought of taking up horse-riding again?'

He laughed. 'No, I've grown out of it. Emma will, too, don't worry.'

'I'm not worried. I think it's good for her. She loves it.'

'It's her age. A craze lots of girls go through. It's expensive, and I don't fancy hauling a horse-box about the countryside, taking a kid to shows. You spend all that time and money and then they discover boys and it's all over.'

'As you discovered girls?' she teased him.

Julian smiled. 'There were plenty of girls on the riding circuit. No, I went to university and got too busy for horses—or girls.'

He pulled her closer and began kissing her again. But when he found the zip at the back of her dress and started to slide it down Lacey pulled away.

'What's the matter?' he asked.

'I thought we agreed,' she said, 'that we'd wait.' She stood up, reaching behind her to close the zip.

Julian stood up, too. 'We haven't set a date for our wedding.'

'I don't think Emma's ready.'

'We can't wait forever, Lacey.'

'You mean *you* won't?'

Julian frowned. 'Can you expect me to?'

Of course she couldn't—didn't. 'But you must realise that after what happened we have to think again.'

'Is this about Emma, or about Tully?'

'Tully?' Lacey stared at him. 'We're talking about Emma!'

'We're talking about us,' Julian reminded her tensely, 'but somehow you seem to have lost sight of us lately. I almost think you see more of Tully than of me.'

'You've always known Tully plays a part in Emma's life!'

'And yours. Do you intend him to continue doing so after we're married?'

'Julian, we agreed—'

'I agreed to Emma seeing her father. Not to my wife swanning off with another man whenever she feels like it!'

Lacey gaped at him. 'It's not like that!'

She tried to explain, to tell him they could work it out, but at some stage in the fraught discussion she realised with a sudden bolt of clarity that her heart wasn't in it.

'You're right,' she acknowledged at last, her shoulders slumping. 'It isn't going to work.'

When she got home she felt drained and dejected. The cosy dream she and Julian had shared had been nice while it lasted, but the problems were too big to surmount—or their love wasn't big enough to surmount them. And somewhere deep within there was a budding resentment against Tully which her conscious mind told her was unwarranted and unfair. But in her heart she knew that she was right. That Julian had been right. Tully had come between them.

She went into the lighted lounge and Tully, holding a half-empty wineglass, rose from one of the fireside chairs. She was almost ready to challenge him with deliberately wrecking her marriage plans.

Then he said, 'You have a visitor, Lacey.' And she saw that he was not alone. With a sick sense of inevitability she turned her gaze to the woman in the other chair, recognising the long, seductively crossed legs, the pink-tipped fingers delicately curled around another wineglass, the pencil-slim figure and slender neck, even before the visitor languidly turned an expertly blonded head and gave her a strangely tremulous smile.

Her heart sinking, she tried to inject some enthusiasm into her voice. 'Francine! What a surprise.'

CHAPTER EIGHT

'I'LL BE going,' Tully offered.

'There's no hurry,' Francine said, 'is there, Lacey? Sit down and finish your drink, Tully.'

'Yes, do,' Lacey agreed coolly. 'I didn't know you were in Auckland, Francine.'

'I just arrived tonight. I'm hoping you'll put me up for a while, actually. There isn't anyone else I can go to at such short notice.'

It was an impulse trip, then. 'What are you doing here?'

Francine took a sip from her wineglass, leaned back in her chair, and said, 'The fact is, I've left.'

'Left?' Lacey echoed blankly. 'Left Christchurch?'

'Lloyd,' Francine told her with an edge of defiance. 'My husband. My marriage.'

Tully went some time later, giving Lacey a peck on the cheek, and accepting a warm kiss on the mouth from Francine, who laid a lingering hand on his arm and said, 'Thank you for listening, Tully. I'm sorry for inflicting my troubles on you.'

'Glad to help,' he responded, and Lacey felt her stomach contract as he smiled down into her sister's eyes. 'I hope you and Lloyd can work things out between you.'

She gave a sad smile. 'I think it's too late for that.'

The crease in his cheek deepened momentarily, and Lacey could have sworn she saw a sudden light in his eyes before he killed the smile.

'Where are the twins?' Lacey asked when Tully had gone.

'With Mum and Dad. When I get myself sorted out

125

I'll send for them. I just had to get away!' Lacey wondered what their parents would make of that, but she didn't get a chance to ask. 'God,' Francine said, 'what a mistake I made when I married that man! We're totally unsuited.'

'At the time you didn't think so. Lloyd seems a nice man, and a good father.'

Francine rolled her eyes. 'Oh, he's that, all right. Sometimes I think he only married me to have a family. Once the twins came along I might as well not have existed, except as a sort of super-nanny.'

For the next hour Lacey listened and tried to look sympathetic while Francine detailed all the woes of her marriage.

Eventually Lacey got to bed, feeling completely wrung out and disgruntled after putting Francine in her room and making up the spare bed in Emma's room for herself.

The main problem, Lacey thought, as she laid her throbbing head at last on a blessedly soft pillow, was that until the arrival of the twins Francine had been accustomed to being the centre of someone's life, first her parents' and then Lloyd's. Giving birth to twins had maintained her lifelong conviction of being clever and interesting, but now they were growing out of the cute, attention-grabbing stage, Francine was approaching her thirtieth birthday, and she was panicking about sinking into some suburban rut.

She should worry, Lacey thought. Francine was still gorgeous, as Tully hadn't failed to notice. He'd scarcely been able to take his eyes off her tonight, and she'd not been unaware of it. Lacey knew the signs: the studied grace of her posture, allowing her skirt to ride up just enough to expose a smooth expanse of thigh, the lift of her head that showed off the feminine curve of her neck, the gleaming sideways glance from under fluttering lashes.

Tully's mouth had acquired an infinitesimal upward quirk at one corner, and his eyes were unfocused, as if he was looking back to a time years ago, when he'd been less adept at hiding his feelings and when, to tell the truth, Francine's feminine wiles had been less subtle.

Lacey remembered it too. She and Francine had grown up in the beach-side suburb of Takapuna on the North Shore, and that summer one of the crowd they'd always spent their holidays with had introduced Tully into their circle. Tully and his mother had a house on the beach front, one of the most expensive stretches of real estate in Auckland.

Since she was fifteen Francine had been experimenting with the effect her blossoming sexuality had on the boys, occasionally singling out one or another for a short time. But once she and Tully laid eyes on each other he simply walked in and took her over, and that was that. Until the night that changed all their lives—Francine's, Tully's... and Lacey's.

She had never known what it was that Francine and Tully had quarrelled about that night.

The party was an outdoor affair held on the lawn between the Cleavers' big Mediterranean-style house and the beach, spilling onto the sand. Francine had innocently assured her parents that Tully's mother would be there. She was, for the first half hour or so, smiling graciously at the young people who arrived and gathered in groups around the barbecue. Tully and a couple of friends cooked sausages and steaks, joshing each other and drinking beer or Coke from cans, while some of the girls set out salads and bread rolls on a picnic table nearby. Then Mrs Cleaver said something to Tully, waved vaguely to the rest of them, and disappeared inside the house.

By ten o'clock the barbecue had been allowed to die. A bunch of boys and girls horsing around on the beach went whooping into the water. Two or three couples slipped off hand in hand beyond the reach of the lights, and several others snuggled into rugs or sleeping bags together on the lawn, kissing and murmuring. Lacey sat on the outskirts of a group trying half-heartedly to sing along to a portable tape player.

Tully and Francine had been swimming. It was Francine's raised voice, carrying clearly across the sand in the silence while someone changed over a tape, that caught Lacey's attention. She recognised the shrill note of accusation but couldn't hear the words.

In the moonlight she saw their glistening, shadowy figures halfway up the beach, Tully with his head back and legs apart, his hands resting on his hips, and Francine, her chin thrust forward as she looked up at him, her arms waving wildly, angrily.

Then Tully suddenly moved one hand in a graphic, slashing gesture of repudiation, and Francine fell back as if she was afraid he was going to hit her. Instead he walked right past her and strode towards the house, with Francine half running in his wake. She grabbed at his arm and he shook off her hand, tossing some remark over his shoulder before resuming his angry stride.

Francine fell back again, then came after him, shrieking, 'Don't you dare call me that! And don't turn your back on me, you arrogant *bastard*!'

Other people turned their heads in curiosity, but Tully went on walking as though he hadn't heard, not altering his pace as he reached the grass and went past Lacey without seeing her, taking the three steps to the house in one long stride and slamming the door behind him.

In the silence that followed Francine stood at the edge of the grass, her pert rounded breasts, scarcely covered by the scarlet top of her bikini, heaving with anger and the effort of almost running on the yielding sand. She stopped there, glared around the circle of fascinated eyes and snapped, 'Well, what are you all looking at?'

There was an electric pause and then one of the boys laughed and strolled over to her. 'Don't you think you're worth looking at, Francine? You look gorgeous in that wet bikini, honey!'

He had a beer can in one hand, and he draped the other arm about her. Dropping his voice, he added, 'And you're double-gorgeous when you're mad!'

Francine's shoulders tensed and she raised a hand as if to fend him off. Then she seemed to change her mind, reaching for the beer can instead. 'I need a drink,' she said, and recklessly drained the nearly-full can, her head thrown back and the taut skin of her throat working as the liquid went down.

Someone gave a surprised, admiring, 'Whoo-woo!' And the other boys laughed.

When Francine lowered the can from her lips she was smiling, her eyes bright as she tossed the empty container over her shoulder and hooked her arms loosely about the neck of the boy who held her. 'Go on,' she crooned. 'Tell me more.'

He dipped his head and whispered something in her ear, pulling her closer. Francine gave him a playful slap on his arm, but she was laughing.

Lacey turned away, and caught a glimpse of Tully standing in the doorway just before he closed the door again, this time very quietly. Everyone else was watching the tableau at the edge of the grass, and she was the only one who had seen him. Uncertainly she glanced back at her sister, but Francine and the young man were moving off to join a group lounging about on towels and blankets and sharing cans of drink.

It wasn't her business, Lacey told herself, forcing her gaze away. Someone handed her a can of Coke, and she said thanks and lifted the tab. Not her business at all. Francine certainly didn't need a younger sister interfering in her love life. She didn't have a lot of time these days for Lacey's opinions on anything, least of all her boyfriends.

Although the two of them had got on well enough as children, they had always been as different as sisters could be, and since Francine had discovered boys they had even less in common. Lacey had quickly become bored with her older sister's fervid confidences about the dramas of young love, and she had shown what Francine regarded as an unfeeling propensity for seeing the current boy's point of view. Francine eventually told her she was just jealous, and stopped confiding in her. Whatever Francine and Tully had fought about tonight, it was unlikely that Francine would tell her sister about it. Not that Lacey wanted to know, anyway.

Half an hour later Lacey was uncomfortably aware that Tully had not returned to the party. No one else seemed to have noticed. Some of his guests were getting noisier, while others—notably the couples who lay about with arms and legs entwined—had grown quieter, and a group huddled in a circle of hunched knees and shoulders were silently engaged in passing round a glowing cigarette. Lacey had repulsed the fumbling advances of a couple of unattached young men. They had only decided to try it on with her because all the more attractive girls were taken, she cynically decided.

Glancing again at Francine, she saw that her sister had donned a sweatshirt over her bikini. Not her own and far too big, it probably belonged to the boy whose broad tanned chest she was leaning against. Her eyes were bright and she was laughing, holding out her hand for another can of beer that someone obligingly put into it, while her companion's hands...

His arms were cradling Francine against his body, and his hands were hidden under the baggy sweatshirt she wore. Lacey looked away. She felt a burning in her cheeks, and a stirring uneasiness. Francine was Tully's girl. They'd been together all summer, inseparable. What if he came out and saw her . . . saw her letting that other guy paw her like that? Was Francine crazy?

She looked towards the closed door of the house. Then unwillingly her eyes were dragged back to her sister. Now Francine was looking up into the boy's face, her tongue peeking between her parted lips, and he was grinning, bending towards her . . .

Lacey jumped up. She marched over to the group. 'Francine!'

The boy looked up first, startled. Francine turned her head to her younger sister, annoyance in her face. 'What?' she said irritably.

'I . . . I need the bathroom,' Lacey said, seizing on the first excuse that came to mind. If she could just get Francine away for a minute, give her a chance to think . . .

Francine frowned. 'You're not a baby, Lacey! You don't need me to hold your hand for you.'

Going hot again, Lacey stammered, 'I don't know where it is. You know the house. Can you show me?'

'Go in the back door and down the passageway,' Francine said shortly. 'You can't miss it.' She hitched herself up and changed her position, sitting cross-legged and no longer half lying across the boy's bare chest, although his arms still circled her waist under the sweat-shirt. She smiled at him, ignoring her sister.

Lacey hesitated, then mumbled, 'Thanks,' and walked away.

She went to the back of the house in case anyone who'd heard the exchange watched, and besides, now she really could do with the use of a bathroom.

She found the door and opened it on a darkened passageway. Her groping fingers discovered a switch and depressed it, and a light on the ceiling flared—and then with sharp pop, died.

Wonderful, she thought, almost ready to give up. Five minutes ago, she reminded herself, she hadn't even thought of needing a bathroom. But now it seemed more urgent than ever. The power of suggestion, she supposed.

Down the passageway. How far down? How long was the passageway? She'd had the merest glimpse of doors on either side, and a staircase at the end. Had there been another door facing her beyond the staircase? She thought there had. Maybe that was what Francine had meant when she said, 'You can't miss it.'

Lacey stepped forward into the darkness, her bare feet silent on cool slate tiles, touching the wall with her fingers to orient herself. They glided across wallpaper, then came to wood, a door frame and a door. Maybe the bathroom was right here. It would be logical, at a beachside house, adjacent to the entrance. She found the handle and cautiously opened the door.

Dimly she could see the outline of a washer and dryer over by the window. The laundry, then. Well, surely the bathroom ought to be next to it.

She closed the door and felt her way further along, more confident now. Yes, here was another door. She found the handle and turned it, pushed it open and took a step inside.

Immediately she was aware that her guess had been wrong. The room was too big, and in the milky wash of moonlight through the slats of the venetian blind on the window she knew that the large, square object beneath it was a bed.

But she didn't realise the bed was occupied until a masculine form rose from it so fast that she gave a muffled, shrieking gasp of fright.

'*Francine*?' he queried sharply.

Tully was striding towards her, a tall, dark shape with his hands held out.

Her heart still racing, she said quickly, 'No, it's Lacey.'

He had almost reached her, but now he stopped as though he'd been shot. 'Lacey?' he repeated, as though he'd never heard the name. And then, 'What the hell are you doing here?'

It was stupid to feel hurt. Of course he was disappointed—he'd thought Francine had come, wanting to make it up with him.

'I'm sorry,' she said. 'I was looking for the bathroom. The bulb's gone in the passage.'

'Has it?'

'It just went out when I switched it on. I'm sorry,' she repeated, and started to back out. 'I didn't mean to disturb you.'

'You'd better use mine,' he said.

'What?' Lacey stopped, confused.

'Use my bathroom,' he said. 'It's over there.' His hand moved in indication.

'You have your own bathroom?' Dummy, she thought. Now he knows for sure that you're not in his social strata. And that goes for Francine, too.

'Yeah.' He stretched out a long arm and she blinked as the room light came on. 'This was the guest suite originally. I've had it since I was thirteen. My mother prefers to have her guests stay upstairs.'

'Oh. I see.'

'Do you?' He looked at her with faint mockery. 'It wasn't convenient for her to have a teenager blundering around up there when she was...entertaining in her bedroom.'

Lacey swallowed, part of her horrified and another part fascinated despite herself. Her own parents lived a most conventional life, and it would never have occurred to her to suspect either of them of having an affair. Of course, Tully's parents had been divorced, according to Francine, since he was twelve. Still, she couldn't help being shocked.

She edged away from him. 'O...over there, you said?'

He nodded, and she found the door and another light switch and shut herself into the small bathroom.

It was quite clean, but a wet towel and a pair of swim shorts hung askew over the shower curtain rail, and a T-shirt was crumpled on top of the clothes hamper by the basin. As she washed her hands she noticed the electric shaver on a shelf under the mirror, with a bottle of after-shave and a black comb beside it. On the wall was a poster showing a naked girl seated with her back to the camera and peeking coyly over her shoulder.

There was a tap on the door and Tully's voice said, 'There are clean towels in the cupboard under the basin.'

'Thanks.' She found one and dried her hands. In the high mirror she looked naked, the sarong she wore over a pair of bikini pants leaving her shoulders bare. She'd wriggled out of the top of her suit after swimming earlier, and left it outside with her towel. Wet, it made the material of her sarong damp and clinging, too. The enveloping garment was actually more modest without it. Her hair was nearly dry, but damp little rats' tails still lay on her shoulders, and she absently rubbed at them with the towel. Over the summer, the sun and salt water had cleared the scattering of pimples she'd had on her forehead and chin all winter, and her skin was lightly tanned and glowing. The one thing that Francine envied Lacey was the way her olive-toned skin turned golden-brown in the summer. Francine's fairer skin burned easily.

Francine also had clear green eyes, not muddy hazel. Lacey grimaced at herself in the mirror, hung the towel on an empty rail by the basin, and opened the door.

The bright light had been switched off but a dimmer one glowed over the double bed. Tully lounged on the rumpled blue and black patterned cover, propped against two pillows, one hand behind his head, the other holding a squat bottle by the neck. In the dark she hadn't noticed that he wore only a faded pair of denim shorts. Probably designer-labelled, she thought. Even if she had never seen the big house, and Tully's raking, shiny red car, so unlike the rattling rust-heaps most of the boys drove, she'd have known that his background was money—money and class.

'Thank you,' she said, rapidly walking towards the door. 'I'm sorry to have disturbed you.'

She was reaching for the handle when Tully said, 'I've locked it.'

She whirled about, her eyes wide with shock, her body poised for flight. 'You've *what*?'

He laughed then, his dark head back, white teeth showing. 'Don't panic, I just didn't want anyone else to come charging in looking for the bathroom.' He lifted a hand, the key dangling from his fingers. 'Here, catch.'

Automatically she held out her hand as he tossed the key towards her, but it touched her fingers and fell silently to the carpet. At school she'd always been the last one picked for team ball games and had earned the name of Butterfingers for her lack of catching skills. Feeling foolish, she stooped and groped for the key, straightening with it in her hand. But as she turned to fit it into the lock he said, 'You could stay if you like.'

She looked at him again, her lips parted in astonishment. 'Stay?' she repeated stupidly.

He gave her an oddly crooked smile, and she realised with sudden insight that he was hurting, badly. 'Keep me company?' he suggested, and proffered the bottle in his hand. 'They say it's not good for anyone to drink alone.'

She wondered how much he had already had. 'It's bad for anyone to drink too much, alone or not.'

He grinned. 'You sound like a school teacher.' Mimicking her tone, he repeated, '*It's bad for anyone to drink too much*... How old are you, anyway?'

Lacey flushed. 'Seventeen,' she said stiffly. 'I don't think you need company,' she added with dignity, and turned again to the door.

'Don't go.' He got off the bed and came towards her, grabbing her hand to bring her round to face him. 'I was teasing. Don't be mad at me, Lacey?' He smiled at her coaxingly, lightly swinging her hand in his, and her bones went mushy even as she said to herself, You idiot, he's manipulating you, he knows exactly how to get round a girl.

It made no difference. She could easily have pulled away from his light hold and he would have let her go. Instead she said feebly, 'I'm not mad.'

He'd stopped smiling, but he still held her hand, almost as though he'd forgotten it. Rather abruptly he said, 'You don't think much of me, do you?' Understandably, his voice held a note of perplexity.

'It can't matter to you what I think,' she said, evading the question. He'd probably hardly noticed she existed, except that her parents had subtly and sometimes not so subtly virtually forced Lacey to go along with Francine to activities like this party, and Tully might have resented her unofficial role of semi-duenna. Both girls tacitly understood that their parents hoped the presence of her younger sister might act as a curb on Francine's behaviour. What they couldn't know was that most of the time their daughters made strenuous efforts to stay as far away from each other as possible. Tonight was the first time Lacey had broken their unspoken pact, and it had been a mistake...

'Why should you think it doesn't matter?' Tully asked her. 'Tell me what it is you've got against me.'

'I don't have anything against you!' she said truthfully and perhaps a little too vehemently. The things that made her so wary of him weren't anything he could help. It wasn't his fault that he was more good-looking than anyone had a right to be, or that he'd been born into money. The unconscious swagger that proclaimed his youthful pride and pleasure in being male was typical of his age group. And the sexual aura he carried with him was as natural to him as breathing. What amounted to lethal male charm in him would be no more than ordinary courtesy in other young men. Not that there was a lot of that about in their young circle. Which made Tully all the more attractive by comparison. He seemed streets ahead in sophistication and gave a false impression of being older than the other boys.

He was smiling again. 'You don't?' he asked. 'Then sit down and talk to me for a while, hmm?'

'I thought you wanted to be alone,' she said, but it was a token objection. Already she was letting him draw her over to the bed and arrange one of the pillows so she could sit beside him while he said, 'Not alone. I've just had enough of that crowd out there for now. But there's something peaceful about you, Lacey. You're always so calm and quiet.'

She was shy and insecure, knowing she couldn't compete with Francine and her friends who, although no more than a year or so older, were light years ahead of her in looks and personality, self-confidence and sexual attractiveness. But she didn't suppose Tully would understand that. Shyness was probably a concept outside his experience. Besides, she couldn't help a tiny glow of pleasure at the interpretation he'd put on her inability to join in the noisy fun, the sexual innuendo and teasing that seemed to come naturally to other girls.

She sat back against the pillow he'd placed for her, with her legs stretched out beside his, ankles primly crossed, and her hands folded in her lap. 'What do you want to talk about?'

'Anything.' He lifted the bottle to his lips and lowered it, then cast her a sideways glance. 'You don't talk much, do you?'

'Sometimes.' She didn't talk a great deal at home— Francine had always been the chatterbox, the vivacious one. Lacey was aware that invitations usually came her way only because of her sister. As far as Francine was concerned Lacey was welcome to tag along any time if she just didn't get in the way. She was useful to lull their parents' concerns, and for that Francine was carelessly grateful.

'So,' Tully said, 'are you going back to school after the holidays?'

Lacey shook her head. 'Teacher's college.'

Tully grinned. 'You'll be good.'

'You mean I've got the manner,' she said wryly. 'Actually, I don't want to be a teacher particularly.'

'Why are you doing it, then?' Tully asked reasonably.

'Because my parents think it's a good idea.'

'You don't want to go to university like Francine?'

'I can't.' She would have liked to but her marks had not been quite good enough for a scholarship, and her parents weren't wealthy. Francine was the bright one; she had coasted through school, always in the top class without even trying. In her last year she'd exerted herself and earned a scholarship and the title of dux, before going on to do an arts degree.

'Why can't you?' Tully asked.

'Because not everyone has money coming out of their ears, like you!'

After a moment he said on a note of curiosity, 'Is that why you don't like me?'

'I never said I don't like you. If I didn't like you, why would I be sitting here?'

'Does that mean you do like me?' he countered swiftly, hitching himself up on his pillow to look at her properly.

Lacey confessed honestly, 'I...I guess I don't know you well enough to say.' She'd been so busy avoiding him she'd not really had a chance to get to know him, she realised.

His smile was amazing. 'Maybe we can get to know each other a bit better tonight.' He raised the bottle in a toast. 'Here's to it.' After taking a swallow or two from the bottle, he wiped it with his hand and held it out to her.

Lacey shook her head.

'You don't drink?'

'Not much. I'm not a teetotaller or anything,' she added. The truth was she had little experience with alcohol and less taste for it.

'Have a sip,' he said, 'just to seal our future friendship.'

A sip wouldn't hurt her. She took the bottle and put it cautiously to her lips.

Warm fire ran down her throat and settled in her stomach. She lowered the bottle, blinked a couple of times, drew a quick breath and said, 'What is it?'

'Napoleon brandy.'

'Isn't that horribly expensive? Where did you get it?'

'My mother's cocktail cabinet. And it's not all that expensive. It should be in snifters, but I wasn't expecting company.'

'It's all right,' she assured him. 'I've never tasted brandy before.'

He grinned down at her. 'Do you like it?'

'I don't know.' The taste had been like cough medicine at first, but the lingering flavour left in her mouth was quite pleasant, and the warming sensation inside her decidedly so.

'Have some more,' Tully urged her. 'It'll help you make up your mind.'

Lacey eyed the bottle doubtfully, but she'd only taken the merest mouthful so far, and she'd been drinking nothing stronger than Coke all evening. Another little sip would hardly send her rolling drunk. She took one, and passed the bottle back to Tully. 'What are you studying at university?' she asked him.

'Accountancy and business administration.' He lifted the bottle again. 'But my father pays my fees. My mother made sure of that. I think the reason she's keen for me to get a degree is that it's costing him thousands.' He drank some more, and passed the bottle back to her.

She heard the acrid note in his voice, and his expression had turned dour. She tipped the brandy to her lips before asking, 'Do they still see each other?'

'Not if they can help it. Dad's in Australia now. He still has a couple of factories in New Zealand, but he lives on the Gold Coast with his girlfriend.'

'They're not married?'

Tully laughed. 'I guess she'd love to marry him, but my father's been burned once.'

'Burned?'

'When he left my mother for his beach bunny, she took him for all she could get.'

'I see. This place...?'

'And the house in Sydney and a cash allowance plus a continuing interest in his business. Having a dependent child gave her a good bargaining counter. The lawyers persuaded her she'd do better financially if she didn't force him to sell everything and split the proceeds. Only my father fixed it so that a lot of it went into a trust fund for me, and she can't touch it.'

'That's nice,' Lacey murmured.

'Nice?' He turned to stare at her as though she'd totally astonished him.

'That he cared about you, wanted to make sure you were looked after.'

Tully said scornfully, 'He didn't do it for me! He did it to spite my mother.'

That was horrible, Lacey thought. But maybe he was just bitter because his parents had split up. 'What makes you think so?' she asked him. 'Just because he's left your mother he can't have stopped loving you.'

'Maybe he never did.' Tully shrugged. 'I hardly saw him anyway, he was so tied up with the business. And since he left I've only seen him once.'

'I suppose if he's living in Australia—'

'He owns two factories in Auckland,' Tully reminded her crushingly. 'He's over here at least half a dozen times a year.'

Lacey fell silent, and he said sarcastically, 'Any more bright ideas?'

'I'm sorry,' she said. 'I was trying to help.'

'I'm not pining for my daddy. I told you, I hardly know him. Anyway, when I'm twenty-one I get a part share in the company. My mother's convinced Dad is doing some creative accounting meantime to milk off all the profit that he can and divert it to the Australian branch.'

'She's accusing your father of cheating?'

'Yeah.' He shifted further down on the pillow and took a long pull from the brandy bottle before handing it to her. 'And she's probably right.'

Lacey couldn't imagine her parents becoming embroiled in anything like that. They hardly ever argued, and when they did it was in a low-key fashion that they tried to hide from their children. She sipped thoughtfully at the bottle, that had been warmed by Tully's hands, and gave it back. 'Is that why you're taking business administration?'

'Clever girl. Of course it'll take me three years to get my degree. And then . . . I take my place in the old family firm.'

'What would you do, given a choice?' she asked him.

'Bum around on beaches,' he said promptly. 'I wanted this summer to last forever, until . . .' He suddenly scowled, his hand tightening on the neck of the bottle.

He was thinking of Francine. 'I'm sure she didn't mean it,' Lacey said tentatively. 'It'll all come right tomorrow, you'll see.'

'You reckon?' He turned to her, disillusion warring with hope in his eyes. His hand touched her cheek and he smiled. 'You're nice,' he said. 'A nice kid.'

'I'm only eleven months younger than Francine.'

'Sometimes you seem older. More mature, anyway.'

'I do?' He'd taken his hand away, but she could still feel its imprint on her cheek. Her body was deliciously warm, tingling with a new, pleasant awareness. It was rather alarming, and she reached out and took the bottle from his hand, swallowing a good mouthful to steady herself and hide her expression from him. By now she'd lost count of the number of times they'd passed it back and forth.

She looked up as a match flared, and saw Tully lighting a cigarette. 'I didn't know you smoked,' she said.

'I don't often.' He drew on the cigarette and removed it from his mouth as he shook the match out and flicked it onto the bedside table. 'Want a puff?'

Lacey looked at it with some suspicion, and he said, 'It's not waccy baccy, just an ordinary cigarette.'

Of course she'd tried a cigarette once, when she was ten. It hadn't been a very agreeable experience. 'No, I'll stick with this, thanks,' she said, cradling the bottle. It felt like an old friend now, a comforter. 'They were smoking stuff outside, weren't they? Have you ever...?'

'Uh-huh. I wouldn't mind a joint now, actually, only I don't have any handy.' He took a lungful of cigarette smoke and blew it out. 'That's probably a bad idea, anyway.'

She thought so too, but didn't want him to think she was a complete prude. 'Why do you say that?'

The cigarette glowed. 'Couple of friends of mine smoke regularly. Most of the time they're spaced out. It rots your brain, you know. They've got scientific evidence now.'

'Yes, I read about it. That thing could kill you, too,' she pointed out.

'One cigarette?' he scoffed. 'Actually, right now dying looks like a reasonable option.'

She sat up then. 'Don't be stupid!' she scolded him. 'Just because you've had a spat with your girlfriend? I never heard anything so *dumb* in all my life!'

Tully looked at her for a second and said, 'Yeah, you're right. No girl is worth dying for.'

'There are plenty more of them out there,' she told him, subsiding back on the pillows. Sitting up had made her head swim a bit; she must have moved too quickly.

He grinned. 'You're beginning to sound like one of the guys. The trouble is,' he added more soberly, 'the other girls aren't like Francine.'

'No,' Lacey admitted, sighing. Francine was special, even she knew that. She'd grown up in Francine's shadow, watching everyone watch her sister. Their parents were entranced by her, and Lacey was sure they'd been disappointed by the brown sparrow who had followed their golden lark. After Francine, who had won baby shows almost from birth, walked and talked before her first birthday, raced past every childhood milestone, and all her life had attracted admiring stares and comments from strangers in the street, Lacey must have been an anti-climax.

The other girls weren't like Francine any more than the other boys were like Tully. The minute the two of them clapped eyes on each other they'd recognised that. And so had everyone else. Francine's parents might hope it was a summer romance that would fizzle out, but for the time being they had accepted the inevitable.

Tully's cigarette burned down and he stubbed it out, then lay back with both hands behind his head.

After a while Lacey realised that she'd almost gone to sleep. She sighed again. The bottle in her hand was nearly empty. They might as well finish it off, she thought muzzily. It felt heavy in her hand, so heavy she could scarcely lift it to offer the brandy to Tully.

He made no response, and she raised herself sluggishly from the pillow and sat up to lean over and peer at him. 'You awake?' she asked softly.

His closed lids slowly opened and he smiled at her.

'It's nearly all gone,' she said, holding the bottle up. 'Want to finish it?'

He didn't take the bottle but curled his hand about her wrist and lifted it that way, draining the remainder of the brandy. 'Thanks, Lacey.' His voice was husky, and he didn't let go of her. His other hand came up and touched her hair where it framed her face, the damp ends falling forward. The back of his hand brushed her cheek, and she felt her eyelids flitter as a faint current of electricity seemed to pass over her skin. 'You've been sweet,' he murmured. His fingers floated down the side of her neck to her shoulder, and she held her breath, expecting them to fall away. 'So sweet,' he said, and his hand was on the back of her neck now, firm and masculine, exerting the merest pressure as his eyes darkened and he drew her towards him.

She closed her eyes just before her lips met his, telling herself this couldn't be real, it wasn't really happening. But oh, she wanted it to...

His mouth was gentle and probing, and when she lost her balance and fell against him she found her hand on a hard naked chest and her heart gave a leap of excitement mixed with an odd kind of delicious fear. Her eyes flickered briefly open, and as if he knew it she saw Tully's black lashes lift, then lower again. He didn't stop kissing her, but now his hands were on her bare shoulders and back, stroking them, stroking her arms and then coming back to her shoulders, holding them while his thumbs made little massaging movements, finding the bones.

She felt her mouth open in surprised pleasure, and the bottle dropped from her fingers, rolling onto the carpet by the bed with a muffled thud. Reflexively she tried to move away and sit up, but Tully's arm went to her waist, and he shifted his body so that she lay on top of him, her thighs nestled between his.

She felt what that did to him, and made a feeble effort at resistance, but she too was gripped by a sudden, half-understood need. When she raised her head he grasped it in both his hands and brought her mouth back to his, making her lips part for him.

Her hands roved blindly, finding the rise of his rib cage, the narrowness of his waist. He must stop, she thought, this couldn't go on, it was too dangerous...

She tried to bring her hands up to push against him, but as she fumbled between their bodies her thumb-nail scraped his nipple, and he bucked under her like a startled colt, giving a low groan.

She managed to free her mouth, gasping, 'I'm sorry, I hurt you.'

His eyelids opened on slashing dark brilliance. His voice was thick and slurred. 'No,' he said. 'Do it again. Please.'

Lacey caught her breath. Her whole body was on fire, waves of heat washing over her. He wanted her—Tully wanted *her*! He felt just as she did, she knew it. His eyes, his taut, passion-darkened face, his body, his hands that were stroking her all over now, finding a way under the loose sarong to slide up her hips and along the line of her bikini pants, were telling her so.

Tentatively she moved her thumb back and forth over the tiny, round nub, and his head went back, his teeth showing as he drew in a hissing breath, the sheen of his eyes veiled beneath half-closed lids.

Lacey smiled, her heart pounding with triumph and delight. She couldn't believe that she had this kind of power; it was awesome. She was Circe, she was Delilah, she was every woman who had ever held a man in thrall to her body. She pressed her lips to his, and felt the heat of his mouth, the eagerness of his tongue, heard the harshness of the breath that she could feel under her clever, exploring fingertips.

Then he moved unexpectedly, still holding her mouth to his, flipping her over onto her back, his left hand going out to grope for the light switch, plunging them into darkness.

Distantly Lacey was glad of that. She didn't want him to open his eyes and be disappointed in what he saw. After a while she realised that a light at the corner of the house was shedding a faint glow through the blind, so she could see the ripple of muscle along Tully's shoulders, the shimmer of his eyes when he lifted his head momentarily and then lowered it again, and she felt his lips hot and open on the curve of her neck.

She had no experience, but she knew what to do because Tully's reactions told her where and how he wanted her to touch him. And wherever he touched her she felt as though sparks were leaping from her skin.

When he lifted his body from hers and she heard the zip of his shorts rasp down she went cold and still and kept her eyes tightly closed, afraid to see him. Then his hands were on her bikini pants, and instinctively she drew her legs together, the cool chill of reason and her fear of the as yet unknown momentarily intruding on her mindless hunger.

Then she felt his lips on her thigh, the softness of his hair brushing the sensitive inner skin of the other leg as he gently eased them apart, and she moaned and gave herself up to whatever he wanted.

What he wanted wasn't long in coming and, after all, it was what she wanted, too. It did hurt a little—although she lied when he asked her. She put her arms about him and held him tightly and wondered if he was crying while he sobbed and shuddered against her, but his eyes were dry when he raised his head from her shoulder and tiredly kissed her again.

'Did you feel anything?' he asked her. 'I'm sorry, wasn't it any good for you?'

'It was lovely,' she assured him. 'I felt . . . it felt wonderful.' It had too, she told herself. She still had a sense of amazed wonder that she—*she*—had brought Tully the magnificent to that pitch of sensation, that she had cradled him to her while he lost control of his body and his emotions, that for a few seconds all his need and desire had centred on her and only her. She knew that the first time for girls was bound to be unsatisfying, and it was no fault of his that she hadn't experienced anything quite so cataclysmic herself. In fact, she was rather glad. It would have been embarrassing, in retrospect, if she had been as totally unrestrained as he.

All the same it was a disappointing aftermath when he heaved a huge sigh, threw himself on his back beside her and went almost instantly to sleep.

She would have liked to follow suit, but as the heat and lethargy left her she sat up in panic, fighting down a wave of nausea. *What was the time?* Her parents had insisted that she and Francine must be home by one.

She fumbled for the bedside light and switched it on, glancing at Tully, but he slept on. The night was still hot, and he had a faint sheen of sweat at his temples and on his upper lip, but Lacey was shivering. She peered at her watch, and took it off to shake it, unable to believe that it wasn't yet twelve o'clock. Hadn't they talked for hours? And then . . . but *that* had taken no more than fifteen minutes, she supposed. Fifteen minutes to change from a girl into a woman, to give away her virginity.

Now she was appalled, and more than slightly sick. *Tully*, she thought. My God, I let *Tully* take it from me! The last person she had expected . . .

And not at all the way she'd ever dreamed . . .

Suddenly it seemed very sordid. She moved to get out of the bed and winced, realising she was sore. And when she stood up she felt dizzy. All that brandy, of course.

She'd been a fool, all kinds of fool. Why had she done it?

She staggered to the bathroom just in time to get rid of the brandy and everything else she'd drunk or eaten during the evening, and afterwards leaned weakly over the basin and rinsed the sour taste from her mouth with cold water. There was no sound from the bedroom. Tully, she guessed, wouldn't wake for ages—he'd seemed dead to the world. She turned on the shower, stripping off the loosened sarong with trembling fingers. *Tully*. Tully and she...

It was unbelievable. Francine would *kill* her if she found out. Supposing Tully told her? He wouldn't! He wouldn't tell anyone, would he? Surely... Oh God, don't let him tell anyone!

He was still asleep when she found the discarded key and crept out of the room. She felt distinctly light-headed, as though she were floating, weightless and not quite in the world.

Everything looked just the same as when she'd left, except that the groups had shifted about a bit, and Francine and the boy who'd been with her had disappeared. No one had even noticed Lacey's absence.

Usually she'd have waited for Francine to come back. Tonight she didn't care. Let Mum and Dad ask questions. Francine could field them. 'Tell my sister I've gone home, will you?' she asked a group of people. They nodded indifferently and she made her way to the sand and along the beach, then onto the road between the houses.

But when she had let herself in and her mother called through the closed bedroom door, 'Is that you, girls?' she answered, 'Yes, Mum.'

'Turn off the light out there and lock the door,' her mother instructed.

She switched off the light and left the door unlocked. Although the night was warm she was shivering, and she pulled an extra blanket from the closet and huddled into her bed. When Francine crept into the house much later, she pretended to be asleep.

CHAPTER NINE

HAVING Francine to stay was rather like housing a cross between an exotic butterfly and a tiger-cat. While Lacey, barefoot and wearing the rumpled oversize T-shirt that was her summer nightwear, was making sure Emma had breakfast and got off to school on time, Francine would arrive in the kitchen with her pale hair gleaming and her makeup already flawlessly in place, wearing an emerald silk wrap belted around her impossible waist and saying, 'I'm dying for coffee! No, *please*, not instant, darling! Never mind, I'll make it.' The last in long-suffering tones. Then she'd proceed to get in the way until the coffee was ready, and by the time Emma had left she'd be sitting at the table with her third coffee, ready to subject Lacey to a lengthy, in-depth analysis of her failed marriage.

On the third day Lacey cut her short with, 'So, what are your plans?'

Francine blinked. 'Plans?'

Lacey spread butter lavishly on a piece of toast and folded the morning paper to the crossword on the back, knowing it was a futile gesture. Usually she finished it over her breakfast before starting work, but Francine's advent had changed that. 'The twins are at school. You could get a job,' she suggested. 'I take it you're not planning to live on the DPB?'

'The Domestic Purposes Benefit?' Francine looked horrified. 'Of course not! Lloyd can afford to pay me maintenance.'

'You may have to take him to court to get it,' Lacey pointed out. 'After all, you left him. And even if he does pay up you won't be able to afford the kind of home and lifestyle you've had with him.'

Francine seemed taken aback for a moment. 'I've got a degree. I'll find a job if I have to.'

'I wish you luck,' Lacey said grimly. 'Even a good degree doesn't automatically qualify anyone for a job these days, especially an arts degree.' Of course, Francine's looks would count in her favour. She handed over the Situations Vacant section of the paper. 'Here, you can start looking.'

'What a bossy little thing you've turned into, Lacey. No wonder Tully says you scare him.'

'*Scare* him?' Lacey snorted. Tully was scared of nothing and nobody. 'He has a weird sense of humour.'

He'd called round the night before, ostensibly to bring a *Geographic* magazine article he'd come across on crocodiles, remembering that Emma was studying them for a school project. But after she'd gone to bed he'd lingered, talking to Francine. After a while Lacey had pleaded a deadline, pleasantly invited Tully to feel free to stay as long as he liked, and retired to her office to abuse her keyboard, because she couldn't stand the faraway smile in Tully's eyes as they rested on Francine's flowerlike face.

'He's scarcely changed, has he?' Francine mused. 'Except that he's even sexier than ever.'

Her eyes had the same glazed look of reminiscence that Tully's had held the night before. Lacey clamped her teeth together so tightly that her jaw ached, fighting an urge to shake her sister senseless. Ducking her head, she picked up the pencil by her plate and scribbled an answer into the crossword. It fitted but she knew it was dead wrong.

Francine said, 'And you still haven't managed to get him to marry you.'

Carefully Lacey unclenched her teeth. 'The offer's open any time I like to take it up,' she said, making an effort to sound casual rather than defensive.

'And you haven't?' Francine looked incredulous for a second, then suddenly comprehending. 'You're probably wise. A man like Tully is hardly likely to be faithful to a woman he married for—well, call it convenience. I suppose it's one thing to be available for the odd romp, but having to turn a blind eye as his wife might be a bit more difficult.'

The odd romp? Lacey swallowed a furious retort. 'Tully and I don't sleep together,' she said evenly.

'What, never?' Francine's brows rose in delicate disbelief.

'Never.'

The disbelief changed to indulgent understanding. 'Mm, you're not his type, really, are you? God, what a fool you were, Lacey. I expect you were just so thrilled that he'd even look at you for a minute, you couldn't help yourself.'

That was so nearly true that Lacey inwardly cringed.

'And in a way you got what you wanted.' Francine's green eyes were strangely cat-like. 'You managed to take him away from me.'

'I never wanted that!'

'Of course you did. All the girls wanted Tully, and you were no different. You always did sulk when you wanted something you couldn't have. When we were kids, where I'd be screaming, throwing a tantrum to get my way, you'd sit in a corner and scowl.'

Lacey almost smiled at the accuracy of the observation. But the smile died when Francine said, 'In fact, any other girl would have done for Tully that night, just to get back at me. And most of them would have had the sense to make sure he didn't get them pregnant. Still, it was clever of you to decide to keep the baby. If it had

been me I'd have got rid of it. I never suspected that
Tully had such a strong paternal streak.'

Tully had never directly suggested she have an
abortion, though his mother had unexpectedly visited
one day and offered to pay for one. Mrs Cleaver had
shown no sympathy, but rather an amused impatience
with what she obviously regarded as a deliberate attempt
at entrapment. She conceded that Lacey had been quite
cunning to have cut out her prettier sister, but made it
clear that no ambitious little lower class slut was going
to become a member of her family, and Lacey needn't
expect any other payment than what the law could force
Tully to provide. She had never shown the slightest
interest in her granddaughter.

'Tully's been a good father,' Lacey told Francine.

'And there's really nothing between you two?'
Francine asked curiously.

'Friendship,' Lacey told her firmly, 'for Emma's sake.'

'Then you won't mind,' Francine asked, her eyes
gleaming, 'if I decide to... renew our acquaintanceship.'

Lacey's heart lurched uncomfortably. 'You're
married!' she said.

Francine looked at her and laughed. 'Separated.
Goodness, you sound like a Victorian grandmother. Like
my husband!' She grimaced. 'I want—I *need* a bit of
spice in my life. And Tully might be just the man to
provide it.'

Tully appeared quite willing. When he came to collect
Emma at the weekend, and suggested they go to the
Maritime Museum as it was raining again and riding
didn't seem a good idea, Francine said, 'Oh, I've never
been there! Is it good?'

'Come along and see,' he invited her, after the briefest
pause and a quick, enigmatic look at Lacey. 'Is it okay
if your Aunt Francine joins us?' he asked Emma.

'Of course it's all right. I hope you like it, Aunty.' She was too polite to say no, Lacey knew. But did she have to give Francine quite such a dazzling smile?

'I'm sure I will.' Francine smiled back at her niece, and Lacey realised for the first time that there was an elusive likeness between them. Some of the genes that Francine had inherited must have been passed on through Lacey to Emma. Emma was going to be lovely when she grew up.

Lacey looked from her daughter to her sister, and felt a tug of regret. Emma, of course, she loved with her heart's blood, but Francine, too, was family. She and Lacey might have squabbled as children and caused each other a great deal of pain when they were teenagers, and grown apart as adults, yet they had shared through the years more than the same parents.

They'd exchanged secrets and silly jokes, discussed childish problems, or simply had fun together. There had been times when Lacey had proudly stood by her parents, wholeheartedly applauding Francine's latest success, admiring her poise, her prettiness, basking in the glow that surrounded her. And times when Francine had casually, if a trifle impatiently, helped Lacey wrestle with her homework, or seen her sister floundering in a social situation and easily diverted attention to herself, allowing Lacey to sink gratefully into the background. A couple of times Francine had taken her in hand and fixed her hair and face for a special occasion, even rifling her own wardrobe for the right accessories.

Last night Francine had put up Emma's hair for her, plaiting and pinning it and allowing some soft curls to fall across her forehead and frame her face.

'Will you do it again for me tomorrow?' Emma had asked. 'So Daddy can see it.'

Francine had, and Tully had duly admired the result. Lacey had felt at first that the style was unsuitable for a ten-year-old. Now she saw that it was simple, youthful and perfectly sensible for an active child.

'I'd love to come,' Francine was saying. 'Lacey, what are you going to do with yourself?'

Lacey was fairly sure Tully had not mentioned Julian to Francine, and she blessed the fact. Questions about him would have been more than she could take. She shrugged non-committally.

Tully said, 'I'm sure Lacey has something in mind. Will it take you long to get ready?'

'Five minutes,' Francine promised. She was back in fifteen, looking stunning in slim fitting jade green pants and matching shirt, with a Burberry raincoat flung over her shoulders. Her hair, too, was pinned up, but on her it looked sophisticated and seductive. Lacey sighed.

Left alone, she tried not to feel lonely and resentful. No doubt Tully assumed she'd have leapt at the chance to see Julian.

Well, the bathroom needed a proper cleaning. She was just in the mood for it.

She was on her knees with her head in a cupboard and scrubbing a shelf when the phone rang. She dried her hands, reflecting that she really ought to invest in a pair of rubber gloves, and went to answer it.

'Lacey? Is Francine there?' a male voice asked. 'It's Lloyd.'

'I'm sorry, she's not in. Shall I get her to call you?'

'Where is she? What's she doing?'

'Um . . . she's visiting a museum with . . . with Emma.'

'A *museum*?' He seemed to be digesting that. 'And she's taken your daughter to see it. Well, you can tell her that *her* daughter's missing her. Her son, too. And ask her when she's coming home!'

'I . . . uh . . . I don't think she's planning to come home,' Lacey said. 'She said she'll send for the children when she's settled here.'

'She doesn't mean it! This whole thing is ridiculous! Nobody leaves a marriage because they're *bored*!'

Francine might. 'Is that what she said?' Lacey enquired cautiously.

'She admitted I'd done nothing wrong, that I've given her everything she wanted.'

Except excitement, maybe. Lacey said, 'She told me she wants some spice in her life.'

'Spice!' Lloyd said contemptuously. 'What's that?'

Suddenly irritated with him, Lacey said, 'You're an intelligent man, Lloyd. It shouldn't be too difficult to work it out. She'll be back this evening. Why don't you phone then?'

She mentioned his call as soon as the others returned.

Francine went cold and glittery. 'I don't want to speak to him,' she said. 'It's been such a wonderfully relaxing day,' she turned to smile at Tully, 'I don't want to spoil it by having a row with Lloyd.'

Lacey relayed rather grittily, 'He said the children miss you.' Francine looked momentarily stricken, her mouth trembling, then she blinked her beautiful green eyes and said, 'That's emotional blackmail. I won't give in to it.'

She might have resented the fact that they'd diverted Lloyd's attention from her, Lacey reflected, but she loved her children. She was inordinately proud of their looks, their talents, their childish accomplishments, and was genuinely missing them.

'I told him you'd be back this evening.'

'Tell him I've gone out again!'

'Lie for you?'

'Lacey, one little white lie! Oh, all right.' Francine threw up her hands. 'If it bothers you I'll go out and make it the truth.'

'On your own?'

'Not necessarily.' Francine turned to Tully.

Responding on cue, he smiled down at her, a spark of devilment in his eyes, and said, 'Where would you like to go?'

Francine laughed delightedly. 'That's what I like about you, Tully. You never miss a beat.'

'You don't have plans for tonight, Lacey?' Tully asked her. 'If you want me to stay with Emma...'

'No. I'd have told you before if I did.'

'That's fine, then,' he said easily.

It was far from fine, Lacey thought, stalking out of the room on the pretence of having to visit the bathroom. If Francine was determined to wreck her marriage he didn't have to aid and abet her. They were acting like a couple of teenagers—as they had when they *were* teenagers?

No, of course not. Both of them had learned to be a bit more discreet about showing their feelings. The raw sexual fire that had sizzled between them was no longer blatantly visible. But was it still there, cloaked under the light chat about old times, the reminiscent smiles, the soft, faintly regretful light in Francine's eyes, the amused warmth in Tully's?

She bent over the basin, splashing cold water on her burning cheeks, passionately hoping that Tully and her sister would be gone by the time she came out.

They weren't, but mercifully they left shortly afterwards, and she made sure she was in bed before she heard Francine open the door with the key Lacey had given her, and the engine purr that told her Tully had driven away.

'We went bowling,' Francine told her next morning over the breakfast table. 'I haven't had so much fun in years.' Her eyes were bright and her normally pale cheeks had a delicate flush. 'Oh, do stop sulking, darling. Did Lloyd give you a hard time when he phoned? What did you tell him?'

'I said you'd gone out with a friend. You never used to call me darling.'

'Don't you like it? You are a darling, though, putting me up like this. I do realise it's a nuisance for you. We haven't always been friends, have we? But I couldn't go to anyone else in the circumstances.'

'We're sisters.'

'Yes. It counts for something, doesn't it? I know I was a bitch after you and Tully... well, when you were pregnant.'

'You were. But I couldn't really blame you. It must have been a hell of a shock.'

'I still can't believe,' Francine shook her head wonderingly, 'that you did it. With *Tully*! I mean, you were *such* a goody-goody. Mum and Dad thought you were going to keep *me* on the straight and narrow!'

'I don't know why. You were older than me, anyway. What could I have done?'

'Nothing, and if you'd tried I'd probably have gone the other way just to show you.'

'Show me what?' Lacey asked blankly.

'Oh, I don't know,' Francine said vaguely. 'That I didn't care, maybe. I was always jealous of you, of course.'

'*What*?' Lacey squawked. What a ludicrous thought!

'Well, it's normal,' Francine said. 'You know, sibling rivalry. You were the baby that displaced me.'

Lacey gaped at her.

'Of course I don't exactly remember your arrival,' Francine said. 'But I know when I was quite young I resented you being there, taking Mum's attention. I think I spent our whole childhood trying desperately to regain that central place in the family that I'd had before you came along.'

'You succeeded,' Lacey said, feeling rather dazed. 'Mum and Dad adored you. I always felt like an unwanted extra.'

'Did you?' It was Francine's turn to look astonished. 'I thought you were so secure, so smug. Serenity, Tully calls it. You never had to strive for attention because as the youngest you got it automatically. And then you got Tully, too...' Francine grimaced. 'I thought I'd never forgive you for that. For the first time in my life I had someone I didn't have to share with you...and then you just took him from right under my nose and it was all over. Not only that, you got all of Mum and Dad's attention.'

'No,' Lacey said. 'They were concerned for you, too.'

'A bit, maybe, but I was just a teenager with a broken heart. They knew I'd get over that. *You* were the one who was pregnant, needing care and support. I felt so left out...' Francine lowered her head, and Lacey realised she was blinking away tears. 'And betrayed...'

'Oh, Francie,' she said. She hadn't used the childhood pet name in years. 'I'm sorry! We were all so young! And I made such a mess of things.'

Francine lifted her head, shaking her hair back, and smiled, brushing at her cheeks. 'It was all a long time ago. And I can't really blame you. Tully was pretty irresistible, wasn't he?'

Lacey nodded. 'It wouldn't have happened, you know, if he hadn't been drinking. Both of us had.'

Francine smiled again. 'Well, never mind. Maybe it will all turn out for the best.'

Lacey's heart sank like a cold, hard stone.

Later Tully took Francine to look at some apartments she'd seen advertised. 'They're having an open house, and since I've got no transport he offered to take me in his car,' she told Lacey. Lacey clamped her lips together and said nothing.

Tully didn't stay when they arrived back, but Francine said he'd volunteered to take her house-hunting again on Monday.

'Don't the real estate agents pick you up if you don't have a car?' Lacey asked.

Francine shrugged. 'I guess, but I don't know anything about buildings and stuff. I'd value Tully's advice.'

Lloyd phoned again that evening. Lacey handed Francine the receiver and she carried it into the bedroom and closed the door, but the sound of her raised voice penetrated to the dining room where Emma was busy with felt-tipped pens and a sketch-book at the table while Lacey caught up on some unfinished work on her word processor. Francine's presence had made it difficult for her to keep to her usual work routine.

When Tully called for Francine the following day she was still in the bedroom—making herself look ravishing, Lacey had no doubt. She herself was wearing a pair of comfortable cotton pants and a T-shirt featuring a snarling tiger on the front, the first clothes she'd laid eyes on in her wardrobe that morning.

Tully eyed the shirt interestedly as she opened the door to him. Apparently he felt that taking her sister out required a different etiquette; he'd rung the front doorbell and waited to be let in. 'Is that a warning?' he asked, his eyes on the tiger motif.

Maybe she'd subconsciously chosen it because of her mood, but Lacey simply said, 'Emma gave it to me. Come in. I don't know how long Francine will be.' Her sister must have heard the bell.

She returned to the dining room-cum-office, not realising at first that he was following.

'You wouldn't like to come with us?' he asked her.

'I've got work to do. I'd have thought you would have, too.'

'One of the perks of being the boss,' he said, 'is the freedom to take a few hours off now and then. I have good people to delegate to.' He leaned against the table, his arms folded.

'One of the drawbacks of being a single-person business,' she replied, placing a hand on the back of her typing chair, 'is not being able to delegate work to someone else.'

He grinned. 'Perhaps you could employ your sister.'

'I don't think it would work. Why don't *you*?'

'I can't think what she could do, besides look decorative.'

'Isn't that enough for you?'

He raised his brows.

Slightly ashamed of herself, Lacey changed tack, saying sharply, 'She has a degree, you know.'

'I keep forgetting.'

Then Francine was in the doorway, saying, 'Oh, there you are. Sorry I kept you waiting.'

Tully turned. 'No problem,' he said, smiling at her. 'You're always worth waiting for, Francine.'

When she heard a car come into the drive later, Lacey assumed that Tully and Francine were back. The doorbell took her by surprise, and when she opened the door she didn't recognise the grim-faced man who stood there until he said, 'Hullo, Lacey. I've come to see my wife.'

A taxi was accelerating away from the house.

'Lloyd,' she said, her nerves jumping with dismay. 'You'd better come in.'

She gave him tea in the lounge, enquired after her parents, and the twins, and tried to make small talk while listening for the sound of Tully's car.

The noise of a passing heavy vehicle must have covered it. Unexpectedly she heard the door open and the sound of Tully's laughter, followed by footsteps in the hallway. Francine walked into the room, saying over her shoulder, 'I don't think I could *live* with mustard yellow wallpaper and...'

Tully was behind her, and as she caught sight of her husband and stopped abruptly in the doorway, he put a hand on her shoulder, their bodies touching.

'Lloyd!' Francine said, and for an instant she seemed to shrink backwards, bringing her even closer to Tully. 'What are you doing here?' She walked forward then, and Tully's hand dropped to his side.

Lloyd's normally pleasant features didn't look at all pleasant now. He looked thunderous. 'I've come to take you home,' he said curtly. Turning to Tully, he snarled, 'And who the hell are you?'

'He's Emma's father,' Lacey said quickly, going to his side. 'Tully, this is Lloyd, Francine's husband.'

'Tully,' Lloyd said, studying him. 'I've been wanting to meet you for a long time.'

'Really?' Tully moved towards him, his right hand going out.

'You're the two-timing bastard who got Francine's little sister pregnant.'

Francine said, '*Lloyd!*'

Tully dropped his hand, his mouth twitching at one corner. 'The very one.'

'Think it's funny, do you?' Lloyd's chin was thrust forward, his hands clenched. 'Think you're clever? Putting a wedge between two sisters? Busting up a family?'

'Not particularly,' Tully said.

'And now you want to do it again!'

'Not at all—'

'Well, not this time,' Lloyd growled. 'Not *my* family. And I'm warning you, if I see you lay a finger on my wife once more, I'll punch your teeth right down your damned throat! Is that clear?'

'*Lloyd!*' Francine's eyes were wide with shock. 'He's a doctor!' she said frantically, her eyes darting from her husband to Tully and then Lacey. 'He doesn't *hit* people!'

'There's always a first time,' Lloyd said. 'And I know where it hurts most.'

'Lloyd!' Francine's voice was fainter this time.

'Understand me, *Tully*?'

They stood almost toe to toe, Lloyd's fists ready to swing, Tully's hands loose at his sides. He was a fraction taller, and certainly broader, but Lloyd's aggressive stance was intimidating.

Lacey glanced at Tully's face and found it quite impassive. Would he stand for being threatened like this without retaliation? She'd never known him to back down from a fight of any kind. He was more likely to bait the man just for the fun of it.

'Tully,' she whispered. She could do without a fracas in her living room.

She saw his shoulders flex, and closed her eyes. Then opened them again as she heard his deep, even voice. 'I understand. Perfectly.'

Lloyd looked into his eyes a moment longer. 'Good,' he said. 'And now, if you don't mind, Lacey,' he nodded perfunctorily in her direction, 'I'd like a word alone with Francine.'

Tully took her arm and guided her towards the door and into the passageway. Turning back with his fingers on the handle, he said, 'Just one thing—you're not planning to use...er...physical persuasion on her, are you?'

'I have never inflicted violence on my wife!' Lloyd assured him stiffly. 'And I'm certainly not likely to start now.'

'Just checking,' Tully murmured, and closed the door. 'Come on,' he urged Lacey, starting towards the kitchen. 'Unless you have a desire to eavesdrop.'

Hastily she followed him. 'Thank you,' she said, 'for not hitting him.'

'You've got it wrong,' Tully told her, leaning against the bench as she automatically filled the coffee maker. 'Lloyd was the one dying to hit *me*.'

'You could have laid him flat on his back and you know it.'

'Thanks—I think. I don't actually go around flattening people.'

'He was goading you.'

'Mm. Maybe I should have let him hit me—he might have let off some steam. It's really Francine he's mad at.' Tully cocked an ear. The sound of raised voices was scarcely muffled by the closed door of the lounge. 'I hope we haven't made a mistake, leaving them alone.'

'I'm sure he isn't the type to attack a woman.'

'You're probably right. Still, I'll stick around.'

'What will you do if she goes back with him?'

'Do?'

'I mean...how will you feel?'

'Relieved,' he answered promptly.

Her gaze flew to his face. '*Relieved*?'

'Something tells me my life isn't safe from Lloyd until she does.'

'It's not a joke!'

'That's what Lloyd said. Do *you* want to punch my teeth down my throat, too?'

'I'm thinking about it!'

He laughed, but when she looked into his eyes she felt her breathing constrict, and involuntarily took a step back. He followed, trapping her against the bench, his hands on either side of her. 'Wanna try it?'

'Don't...don't be silly,' she said, putting her hands against his chest to push him away. He didn't move. 'Tully...'

'Of course,' he said, 'I can't promise I won't retaliate. I might,' he added, his voice low and lazy, 'even lay you flat on your back...eventually.'

'*T-Tully*!'

His laughter now was soft, seductive. He leaned forward, blowing a wisp of hair away from her temple. She felt the warmth of his breath on her skin.

'Stop it!'

He moved away, lifting his hands, but she remained against the bench, afraid her legs might not carry her.

'Saving yourself for Julian?' he taunted.

'Julian?' Of course, she still hadn't told him. 'Julian and I...we decided to call it off. We're not getting married.'

His brows shot up. 'You're not?'

If he hadn't looked so pleased she wouldn't have got mad at him. But the unholy grin that spread across his face was his undoing.

'You *bastard*!' she snarled at him. 'You don't give a damn about anyone, do you? Except yourself and maybe Emma.' She'd thought he had some genuine feelings for Francine, that something between them had endured all these years. 'You can't even be bothered fighting for Francine, can you?'

'Is that what you want me to do?' he demanded. 'Help her to wreck her marriage?'

If that had stopped him, then possibly he'd been considering more than his own immediate pleasure. Irrationally, the thought gave her a sickening jolt. 'You really care about her?'

'I don't give a hoot in hell about Francine!' he said angrily.

Lacey stared at him. 'Then what's been going on between you two ever since she got here?'

'Going on?'

Almost shouting, Lacey said, 'Don't put on that innocent act with me! Do you think I haven't noticed the soulful "Do you remember?" looks you've been giving each other? The two of you have been behaving like a couple of love-struck teenagers! It's...it's...'

'Disgusting?' Tully suggested helpfully.

'*Pathetic*!'

'Ouch!' But now he was grinning again. 'You sound,' he said with great satisfaction, 'like a jealous shrew.'

It was too much. She launched herself at him, incoherent with rage, grabbing a couple of handfuls of his shirt, trying to shake him. Of course it had no effect at all; he was as solid as a kauri tree. 'I am not *jealous*!' she panted. 'I'm *furious*!'

He plucked her hands away, capturing them in his. 'I can see that,' he said and, apparently quite seriously, added, 'Why?'

She pulled away, but it was no use trying to free herself. She glared at him instead, and found his eyes intent and questioning, with no hint of laughter in them at all. '*Why*, Lacey?' he asked quietly.

'Because everything's a game to you! I thought you wanted Francine, but when Lloyd arrived you just walked out with hardly a backward glance. I *know* you don't want me, but you deliberately set out to wreck my relationship with Julian—'

'That's not true.'

'It *is*!' she insisted. 'You tried to sabotage it from the time I first told you about him.'

He seemed to be thinking something over. '*That* part's true enough,' he acknowledged. 'Almost. I wasn't going to just step aside and let him walk off with you—'

'No, you couldn't, could you? You had to prove that no man can compete with you. You couldn't stand the thought of anyone taking what you didn't even want yourself! Well, I'm not your property, Tully! You can't put up No Trespassing signs—'

Suddenly he had released her hands, swearing so loudly she jumped. Turning to the bench, he slammed both hands down on it, then turned to face her. '*Damnation*, Lacey!' he yelled. 'How many times have I asked you to marry me?'

She blinked at the raw fury in his face. 'What's that got to do with anything?'

He took a step towards her, looking so menacing that she backed away until she found herself hard up against the table. '*Why* do you think I *wanted* to put up a No Trespassing sign? Why the *hell* do you think I tried to prove to you that you didn't really want to marry Julian? Why *should* I be moving heaven and earth to make you see he isn't the right man for you? Haven't you ever wondered about that?'

'You didn't want your nice comfortably arranged life to change, and besides, you were having fun,' she said bitterly, 'goading Julian, teasing me—'

'Fun?' Tully sucked in a quick breath, raised his eyes at the ceiling and then glowered at her. 'You think *fun* was all it was about? Didn't it ever occur to you that it might have something to do with *wanting* you? *Loving you*?'

Lacey blinked. 'You don't—'

'The hell I don't!' An arm snaked about her waist, yanking her against him. His mouth came down on hers as his other arm went about her shoulders, holding her firmly while he kissed her with savage passion, a dizzying mixture of anger and desire that stopped her breath and sent her heartbeat into overdrive.

After a while he must have realised that she wasn't fighting him, and the kiss became less overpowering but still as sexy as hell. He kept exploring her mouth as if he'd never get enough of it, as though it was the most fascinating, important thing in the world, as though...as though he loved her.

The thought made her shiver, and he raised his lips at last from hers and said huskily, 'If you tell me you ever kissed Julian like that, I'll wring your neck.'

She smiled rather tentatively into his glittering eyes. 'No, you won't.'

'*Lacey*!' His voice grated deep in his throat, and his brows drew together threateningly.

'Lacey!'

Francine. She'd totally forgotten about Francine, about Lloyd. Gasping, she pushed against Tully's chest, and this time, after a moment when she thought he wasn't going to budge, he loosened his hold and let her turn to her sister in the doorway, although his arm remained about her shoulders.

'We're leaving,' Francine said, her gaze taking in their flushed faces, a surprised, rather put-out look on her face. 'I thought you said...?' She eyed Lacey accusingly.

'What?' Tully asked.

'Never mind,' Lacey said hastily. 'Is everything all right?'

'No,' Francine admitted. 'But we've talked about a few things, and we'll talk some more at home. Maybe get some marriage counselling. I didn't think Lloyd cared enough to come after me—it wasn't easy for him to make the time for it. And I had no idea that he'd...well, that he felt so strongly about me.' She glanced at Tully. 'I can't believe he actually threatened you!' she said in tones of wonder.

'I hope things work out for you,' Tully said politely.

'You, too.' Her quizzical look encompassed both of them. 'It was nice seeing you again, Tully. Thanks for everything.'

'My pleasure.'

She gave him a slow, provocative smile. She can't help it, Lacey thought resignedly. They are two of a kind, she and Tully. 'Not as much as it might have been,' Francine said softly, 'but thanks for that, too.'

Lacey stiffened, and felt Tully's fingers tighten on her shoulder. 'Your things—' she said to Francine, and walked forward so that he had to let go.

'Lloyd's taken my bags to the car. He asked me to say thank you and goodbye for him. No, don't come out with me. I guess you and Tully have things to talk about, too,' Francine said meaningfully. She hesitated for a moment, then leaned over and kissed Lacey's cheek. 'We must keep in touch.'

CHAPTER TEN

As soon as she heard the front door close Lacey whirled about, demanding, 'Did she make a pass at you?'

Tully's mouth twitched. 'Not in so many words.'

'But she made it clear she was willing,' Lacey said bluntly. 'How could you resist? You can't tell me the spark wasn't still there.'

He looked pensive and a trifle wary. She thought he was going to deny it outright. 'A faint spark,' he said. 'A remembered spark. Blowing on it would have killed it rather than rekindled the flame.'

'Ten years ago—' Lacey swallowed, remembering the incandescence that had hung about them, the blazing attraction that had flared at their first meeting and burned that entire summer.

'Ten years ago,' Tully said, 'Francine and I were a couple of bundles of adolescent hormones. But that's all it was. We were both too self-absorbed and far too immature to have any idea what loving really meant. That's what those "Do you remember?" looks were about. We were laughing at each other—at ourselves.'

'She wouldn't have minded taking up where you left off, though.'

He shrugged. 'Maybe she flirted with the idea, but not too seriously. What she really wanted was Lloyd's attention.'

He was probably right there. Francine might have marked Tully out for her 'bit of spice' when she was feeling neglected and rebellious, but she'd very likely have regretted having an affair with him. As things were,

170

Lloyd had been made aware of the possibility and had reacted, Lacey suspected, in a way exactly calculated to convince Francine her marriage might be worth saving.

'When you were teenagers—'

Tully said impatiently, 'People do grow up, Lacey.'

She had grown up all right, in a big hurry, when she was seventeen.

And as for Tully—

She looked at him, and it was like seeing a stranger. He was a man, broadshouldered and lean but without the youthful swagger he'd once had, the air of taking on the world just for the hell of it. His face was grave and a little tense, and for the first time she noticed that the fan of lines about his eyes didn't entirely disappear when he wasn't smiling.

She'd never stopped thinking of him as a boy, never taken him seriously as a man. And yet, ever since their disastrous teenage sexual episode he'd been making adult decisions, taking adult responsibilities.

She thought of the way he'd dealt with Lloyd's unexpected belligerence. He'd defused the situation, retired gracefully, but made sure that Francine wasn't in danger and stayed nearby to rescue her if necessary. And he'd handled Desma and her unsavoury boyfriend in much the same way—not by violence or empty threats but with intelligence, good sense and impressive authority. She'd always known, she realised, that if she needed him Tully would come through.

'I'm sorry,' she said.

'Sorry?' She was unprepared for the sudden loss of colour in his face, the light dying from his eyes. 'You're not going to turn me down again? You can't! You just *said* you're not marrying Julian!'

'Well, I'm not so desperate I'd marry just anybody!' she said tartly. He really was the limit.

'Am I *just anybody*?' he demanded.

'No.' He was Tully, and she loved him so much it made her ache to think about it—and terrified to remember that she might have married Julian and come to see too late what a horrendous mistake she'd made. She didn't even know when she had begun to love Tully this way—surely not that long time ago when they had been so young and so reckless.

'But,' she objected cautiously, 'all those times you proposed to me, you didn't even pretend it was for love.'

A furrow appeared between his eyebrows. 'Do you think I'm pretending now?'

Uncertainly, she shook her head. He'd said he loved her. He'd certainly kissed her as if he did. But—Tully? Tully, who could have had Francine, who could have had any woman he wanted, and had, she was sure, taken a good many of them to his bed? Could he really be in love with *her*?

'If I marry you,' she warned him with sudden ferocity, 'any time I catch you kissing another woman like that, *I'll* wring *your* neck!'

The light was coming back into his eyes. 'If?' he said. 'Is that a yes?'

'I suppose it must be.'

She thought he'd sweep her back into his arms and kiss her into forgetting any doubts. Instead he took her hands in his and said quietly, 'I know it wasn't love the first time I proposed. But I've been falling in love with you ever since the night we made Emma. You kept me at arms' length ever afterwards, and I can certainly understand why.'

'You can?' Had he known all these years how hard it had been to fight his insistent attraction?

'I was young and selfish and drunk, and I know I hurt you. It must have been pretty horrible. And when I tried, years later, to rectify some of the damage, you thought I just wanted to exploit you.'

Lacey bit her lip, remembering. 'It was something my father said, but I should never have believed it of you.'

'At the time I was fuming, of course. After I'd calmed down I wondered if it was really an excuse, if the truth was that you were afraid sex was always going to be disappointing and painful.'

The truth? The truth was, she'd been so scared of capitulating to his sexuality and getting her heart thoroughly broken, she'd been ready to believe anything that would help. But how could she tell him that?

'That's when I started to really love you,' Tully said slowly, 'to want you. You looked so fierce and so hurt and so sexy, I had this mad urge to grab you and throw you back down on the bed and make you love me back.'

It wouldn't have been hard, she thought. She'd probably have succumbed without a murmur.

'Fortunately I did have some sense of decency left,' he said. 'After that night, I thought I'd have to be content with what you were willing to give. Friendship, and a place in your life... and Emma's. I looked forward so much to the weekends, when I'd bring Emma home and you'd be waiting for us. And the times when you invited me to stay for dinner and afterwards we'd sit by the fire, or out on the porch steps, and maybe not even talk much.'

'I always thought you'd be bored.'

'Bored? I was never bored. Didn't you notice how reluctant I was to go home? I only felt really happy when I was with you.'

Lacey swallowed. She'd been so sparing of invitations, afraid he would accept out of guilt and a sense of obligation. Afraid of making him feel trapped.

He took a deep breath. 'And then you broke the news about Julian,' he said, almost spitting the name. 'And I knew then it wasn't marriage or sex that you didn't want. It was just...me. You simply couldn't bear the thought of sex with *me*.'

What a blow that must have been. Looking down at their linked hands, she said, 'It wasn't horrible that first time, Tully. Maybe not as wonderful as it might have been. But definitely not horrible.'

His fingers tightened. 'Lacey, next time I take you to bed, I promise I'll do my damndest to make it wonderful.'

He let go her hands but only to put his arms around her, bringing her close. And that was how Emma found them when she opened the door.

'What are you doing?' she asked interestedly.

'I'm asking your mother to marry me,' Tully said. 'And this time she had better say yes.'

Emma drew in a huge breath, her eyes going wide and brilliant. '*Say yes!*' she ordered Lacey.

'I already did,' Lacey protested, as Tully laughed low in his throat. 'Didn't I?'

'I want a yes for every time I've asked,' he told her, 'and preferably in front of witnesses.'

'Yes, yes, yes, yes, yes and yes,' she said. 'Satisfied?'

'Never.' His eyes glinted wickedly, his voice a caress.

'Am I a witness?' Emma asked, dancing over to them.

'Definitely,' Tully told her. 'And you'll be a witness at our wedding, too. Okay?'

'*Okay!*' She threw her arms about him as he loosened his hold on Lacey. 'Then you'll be my *real* daddy, won't you?'

'You bet I will,' he said, returning her embrace. Over her head his eyes met Lacey's. 'We're going to be a real family.'

It was what he'd tried all along to provide for Emma, Lacey realised. What she hadn't seen was that it was also what he needed for himself.

*   *   *

It was Emma who insisted they have a proper honeymoon. She had been direly disappointed that Lacey wasn't going to wear a long white dress with a veil and all the trimmings, but had reluctantly approved the heavy apricot silk that her mother opted for. Her own dress was a deeper apricot shade given an old-fashioned look by a wide sash, and both of them wore floral wreaths in their hair. Lacey's parents had offered to stay on after the small, quiet wedding and look after Emma while her mother was away.

For three weeks Tully had been wooing her with flowers and kisses. The house was filled with the scent of roses and carnations. He'd treated her to expensive restaurant meals and a glittering, extravagant imported show. One night he'd taken her to a nightclub and discovered that she liked dancing, and what's more was good at it, though she'd felt self-conscious and out of practice. Tully's confidence, though, soon boosted her own and she'd thoroughly enjoyed herself.

And he'd kissed her—long, drugging kisses full of sweet promise. And murmured more promises, of what he intended to do when their lovemaking encompassed more than kisses, the words flooding her body with heat and making her tremble with anticipation. But he made it clear that in the meantime kisses and promises were all she was going to get.

'This is going to be no shotgun wedding,' he had declared virtuously. And when Lacey raised her brows in surprised query, 'We're not risking conceiving *another* baby out of wedlock. Think how shocked Emma would be. Not to mention your parents.'

'There are ways,' she pointed out, slightly bemused but not too serious.

He ran a slow gaze over her. 'Don't tempt me, woman. I'm having enough trouble controlling my animal appetites as it is.'

It wasn't untrue, she knew the signs of his physical arousal, and yet a small niggling doubt remained that she'd tried ruthlessly to quell.

She'd told Tully that she'd like to spend their ten days' holiday at a beach, thinking of a modest cottage or a motel unit. When he told her to get a passport she'd said, 'But I didn't expect—'

'I know,' he said. 'You never expect enough. I'm not taking you someplace where you'll be cooking and cleaning on your honeymoon! Buy yourself a couple of pretty dresses, too. We're going to be dancing every night—before we go on to other things...' His eyes kindled, resting on her with blatant anticipation.

Lacey had expended what she considered an exorbitant amount on the 'couple of pretty dresses' and also on some positively sinful nightwear and underwear, all satin and lace and sexily cut. She'd never been so extravagant in her life. More than anything she wanted Tully to find her desirable, not to be disappointed in his bride.

Now she found herself in a luxury hotel in Western Samoa, overlooking a beach with palm trees waving in a tropical breeze and tiny islets floating on lazy turquoise water turning pink in the light of the setting sun.

His arms slid about her waist, and she felt his lips nuzzle her nape. 'How are you feeling?'

'Stunned,' she said. 'I can't believe I'm really here, with you. I'm tempted to pinch myself.'

'You're not the only one. These last three weeks I've been scared stiff you'd call it off, after all.'

'*Me*? If anyone was to call it off, I'd have thought it would be you.'

She felt the sudden intake of his breath, before he altered his hold, gripping her arms to turn her. 'Why the hell should I? You still thought I didn't mean it?'

He scowled. 'You have to believe *now* that I was serious about marrying you. About loving you!'

'It's all right, Tully,' she said. 'I know you love me.' He might not love her with a boy's first flush of passion, but what they had was better, surely—deeper and more abiding. 'I love you, too.' More than she dared to let him know.

'Dammit, that's how *you* talk to Emma!' he said wrathfully. Something changed in his face, in his eyes, and he added, 'Maybe I've been using the wrong tactics after all.'

He jerked her forward into his arms with none of his usual finesse, and held her so tightly she could scarcely breathe, his mouth descending on hers with a ferocity that forced a silent gasp from her lips, parting them to a sudden, overwhelming invasion.

He gave no quarter, and she ought to have been furious at his onslaught. She *was* furious, she told herself as her hands wound into his hair. *Furious*, she assured herself as her body arched instantaneously against his, catching fire from the heat that radiated through his thin shirt. Furious, her mind reiterated, while her mouth opened under his like a parched desert flower under rain, and drank him in, and she heard herself moan deep in her throat, returning his kiss with a strange, wild ferocity of her own.

They were both panting when he released her mouth at last. 'I'm sorry,' he muttered. And then, as though he couldn't help himself, he was kissing her again with the same desperate desire.

She felt her own desire mounting, meeting his, and soon his hands were pulling her new silk blouse from the band of her skirt and exploring her back, his thumbs skimming her rib cage, finding the satin covering over her breasts. Lacey gasped, and shivered in his arms.

Then his mouth was on her throat, burrowing into the low neckline of the blouse, pressed to the hollow between her breasts.

She lifted her hands to undo the buttons for him, and he said reluctantly, raising his head, 'You'd better not do that, darling.'

Her fingers stilled, a faint chill stiffening her spine and cooling her heated skin. 'Why not?'

His eyes were dark and glittering, his voice husky. 'Because if you do I won't be able to stop. And I had planned a candle-lit dinner... dancing... maybe a stroll on the beach in the moonlight...'

'Don't you dare stop now!' She glared at him and, holding his surprised eyes with hers, defiantly undid the buttons one by one, while he watched. Then, her hand in his, she led the way to the bed.

It was wonderful. More than wonderful. His lips, his tongue, his hands, worshipped her body in a way it had never been worshipped before. When she said, 'I'm too...' he answered,

'You're perfect. Just perfect... all woman, beautiful, soft, curvy woman.'

When she protested, 'You can't like...' he laughed low in his throat and said,

'I don't, I love it. But if you don't like it...?'

'I love it too,' she assured him, the words coming out in a little gasp. 'Don't stop!'

'I won't,' he promised, 'except for this...'

And that was even better. 'Oh,' she said, 'I didn't know...'

'I did. I knew that with you it would be this good, this great. Like it was for me, the first time. No—better. Slower. I've always wanted to make it like that for you.'

She knew she shouldn't believe that. She didn't believe it. 'I suppose you closed your eyes and pretended I was Francine.'

He stopped dead, his hands ceasing their erotic movements and she thought, I've spoiled it all.

'No! You're nothing like your sister!' he said, his voice harsh. 'You never were.'

'Well, it hardly mattered who I was that night, anyway,' she said, trying to sound sensible about it. 'It was Francine you really wanted.'

He drew in an audible breath, and hitched himself up on the bed to hold her eyes with his. 'I was crazy for Francine—all the guys were. I was a *boy*, and she was everybody's adolescent fantasy. A walking, talking centrefold. But it was you I wanted that night when you came to me. You I...needed. Your compassion, your generosity, your quietness. And your wonderful sexuality—that combination of shy innocence and lushness.'

Her eyes flickered away, but he didn't stop. 'Even then,' he said, 'I think I knew that Francine would never be capable of such abundant giving. Not just sexually— in every way. When we talked, you really listened, and cared. Understood. I learned more about you, and about myself, in the hour or so we spent together in my room than I had about Francine in the entire summer. That was when I started—dimly—to realise that real lovemaking, adult lovemaking, was more than just a physical release or a bit of fun. And the longer I knew you, the more I found myself remembering how it was with you, wanting to experience it again.'

His eyes had darkened with memory, gentled. She hadn't spoiled it after all. His hand resumed its tantalising, arousing journey of discovery, and his eyes roved over her near-nakedness.

She said uncomfortably, 'I could never compete with Francine.'

He shrugged, as though it didn't matter. 'Why would you want to? She's probably as self-centred in bed as she is out of it.' He spoke almost absently, one finger finding a tiny heart-shaped mole just below her left breast. 'That's pretty,' he said. 'Have you always had it?'

'Yes.' She'd never regarded it as pretty, rather as yet another flaw. She felt a melting warmth at the thought that he liked it.

His finger was moving lazily in another direction, sending delicate tingles along her limbs. Before she lost the ability to speak, she said breathlessly, 'What do you mean, *probably*? You and she—you were together all that summer!'

He lifted his gaze reluctantly, with a hint of impatience. 'Didn't you know...? She was a thorough little tease. What do you think we fought about that night? Francine knew exactly how to keep a guy dangling, panting for what she wasn't willing to give. *That* was what excited Francine.'

Of course, she thought, in a moment of revelation. It was the tension, the frustration and uncertainty of fierce, unfulfilled passion pulsing about them that had given them that crackling sexual aura.

'Oh!' she said as he dropped his gaze from her eyes to follow the path of his hand. And then, as his magical fingers found a spot they hadn't yet explored, '*Oh*! Tully...I don't think I can wait much longer...'

It had, after all, been ten years. But when he came to her she remembered the feel of him, the way he'd wrapped himself so closely about her, the warm texture of his skin sliding against hers, how it had been having him hard and deep inside her, and how he'd whispered to her that she was lovely and made her believe it.

But this time was even better. She was floating on dark exquisite wings of desire, then plunging into a maelstrom of hot, spinning sensation, an excitement that built and exploded, and slowly returned her to tranquillity, her cheek on Tully's gently heaving chest.

For long minutes she lay there in silence, a lovely lethargy invading all her limbs while his breathing steadied and his hand played idly with her hair. She closed her eyes and savoured the scent of him, the slight dampness of his skin as she lazily stroked it.

'We'll need a bigger house,' he said.

Lacey opened her eyes. 'What?'

'We want more children, don't we? Do you realise you could be pregnant?' He turned his head, his eyes gleaming. As her eyes widened and her mouth parted, he added, 'Will you mind? Should I have...?'

'No. I don't mind.'

'I've waited so long for this.' He turned his head and kissed her temple contentedly.

Lacey smiled. If he wanted to persuade her—or himself—that he'd been pining for her with unrequited passion, she wasn't going to argue.

'Why are you looking like that?' He regarded her with deep suspicion.

'Nothing.' She stirred, pretending to be looking for her clothes.

He grabbed her arm and made her face him, looking into her eyes as if trying to read her thoughts. He must have gained some inkling of them, because he said at last, 'I'm no saint, Lacey—there were women, you know that. After that fiasco when you accused me of setting you up in a love-nest, I made myself abide by your rules.'

'Was it really that hard?'

'Yes, it was hard!' He frowned at the scepticism in her voice. 'But that was what you wanted and I forced myself to go along with it. And then—' he turned an angry gaze on her '—you told me about Julian. And I wanted to kill him.'

Lacey blinked.

'I tried to be noble about it, reminded myself I owed you some happiness and if I loved you I'd step aside, etcetera. But—'

He stopped, shaking his head, and Lacey prompted him. 'But what?'

'You kept saying how *nice* he was, as if that was the most important thing. It felt all wrong. When I came on the two of you kissing, you might have been exchanging a handshake for all the heat you generated between you. I knew what you were capable of—had been capable of—and I couldn't see you being happy with a guy who didn't even make your eyes light up when he kissed you.'

She was sure her eyes lit up when Tully kissed her. And he'd known it, too.

'And what's more,' Tully said, 'you told me that when Emma was happy, you were. Neither of you was likely to be happy living with Julian. You're both positive personalities, and he's...negative.'

'So you decided to put a spanner in the works,' she suggested, not without a faint spurt of remembered indignation.

'I've never been the self-sacrificing type,' Tully confessed. 'Maybe if I'd been convinced he was good for you, and for Emma, I might have managed it. But when *I* kissed you and you kissed me back with much more fire than I'll bet Julian had ever aroused, I knew that you wanted me, even if you weren't prepared to admit it. And I sure as hell still wanted you. I decided I wasn't giving you up without a fight.'

'And from then on it was no holds barred,' Lacey murmured.

'I was fighting for my life. Our life. You're not sorry, are you?'

'No!' She wasn't sorry.

'God, Lacey, I love you so much. *Adore* you! I'd crawl over broken glass on my knees this instant if you asked me to!'

'I can't think why I should,' Lacey said. 'It would make an awful mess of the rug, and bloodstains are so hard to get rid of.'

'You wouldn't have to clean it up. That's what they have staff for.' He scowled suddenly, and gave her a little shake. 'Why are we discussing this? I'm *serious*!'

He was. She looked into his eyes and saw questioning anxiety in them, the burning sincerity, the lambent desire that their lovemaking had not quite quenched. And she began to believe him.

It wasn't true that he'd never look at another woman. Leopards didn't change their spots, and he'd probably still be eyeing attractive women when he was eighty. But while she lived, looking was all he'd be doing. He might be a leopard, but he was *her* leopard, from this day forward. Hers because he loved her with a deep, abiding love, the kind that lasted for a lifetime, she realised with awe and a glow of pride, of exhilaration, as the reality, the truth of his declaration penetrated her soul.

She didn't want to cage him, but he'd given her the right to call him back if he strayed. 'Did you deliberately set out to make me think you wanted an affair with Francine?' she asked sternly.

He grinned. 'I hoped you'd feel the way I felt when you told me about Julian. It worked, too.'

Lacey tried to be indignant at his tactics, but right now indignation was hard to muster. 'You told Francine you were scared of me.'

His eyes gleamed at her. 'I didn't like to say she just doesn't turn me on any more. And you *were* giving me some pretty fierce looks.'

'So you told her . . .?' Lacey took a heaving breath of her own. 'No wonder she didn't believe we weren't sleeping together! You *fink*!'

'We *are* sleeping together, now,' he pointed out. 'For the rest of our lives.' He leaned back on the pillow with his free hand behind his head, his eyes wandering, the lids drooping sexily while his lips curved into a lazy grin. 'I've figured out the message on that tiger T-shirt of yours.'

'There is no message.'

'Yes, there is. It's not a tiger, it's a tigress, isn't it? Like you—' His voice lowered suggestively.

She gave him a withering look and, to hide the fact that she was blushing like a schoolgirl, began hunting in earnest for her clothes. 'We haven't even unpacked yet,' she said briskly. 'And you said something about dinner?'

'Hungry? I might have known that once you'd had your wicked way you'd discard me like an old glove.' Reluctantly he reached for his trousers.

'I suppose I might as well not have bothered buying nighties,' Lacey grumbled. '*I* had plans for tonight, too.' She'd pictured herself enveloped in sexy satin and a cloud of perfume, welcoming him into their bed.

'Nighties?' Tully sounded intrigued. 'Black lace?' he asked hopefully. 'You'd look terrific in black lace.'

She'd found her blouse and hauled it round her. 'One of them is black lace,' she admitted. 'You'd better make the most of it, because I don't think I can wear it around Emma.'

Tully grinned as she pulled on her panties and stood up to go and rummage in a suitcase. 'Our new house will have more privacy for us—our own bathroom, for one thing. Did I tell you, there's a place for sale at Wiri? It goes to auction the day after we get back. Thirteen acres with a big house on it. Emma could have the cousins to stay, and there'll be her brothers and sisters, of course.'

'Are you going to spoil them all like you spoil Emma? This thirteen acres, it's just so she can own a horse, isn't it?'

'It's so we can own a home,' he said, standing up to zip his pants. 'One we can live in together. One we'll still be living in together when Emma and the other dozen or so have grown up and left home, and it's just you and me for the first time in our lives. I'm looking forward to that.'

'Looking forward to growing old?'

'With you.'

'And I had you pegged as the eternal Peter Pan,' she said.

Tully shook his head. He had his shirt on now but it hung open over his chest. 'Grown-ups have more fun,' he said, casting a wicked glance at the tumbled sheets. 'Don't they?' He strolled over to her and pulled her close, his hands linked behind her waist.

'Yes,' Lacey agreed, smiling back and beginning to button his shirt for him. She didn't need to remind him that it wouldn't be all fun and games, that this was only the beginning of the hard part. Both of them were grown-ups now. They'd weather whatever life threw their way, and sometimes it wouldn't be any fun at all. Grown-ups knew that life wasn't all roses and champagne. But they also knew that having fun, sharing laughter, was an essential part of loving, of life itself, as necessary as commitment and responsibility and willingness to work at a relationship when it seemed to be going wrong, all those things that were implicit in the marriage vows.

A sudden warmth filled her, a delicious excitement at what the future held for them—a lifetime of laughter and tears, of sharing joys and sorrows, of growing together and growing old, of loving. There was light and shade, and right now she and Tully were standing in the sunshine.

HARLEQUIN ◆ PRESENTS®

FORBIDDEN!

It shouldn't have been allowed to
happen—but it did!

#1872 DESERT MISTRESS
by Helen Bianchin

Kristi's brother was a hostage and only one man could
help: Sheikh Shalef bin Youssef Al-Sayed. He had power
and influence at his fingertips—how could Kristi win his
support? He was way out of her league....

Available in March wherever
Harlequin books are sold.

FREE VALENTINE'S BROOCH!
$9.95 U.S. retail value

This Valentine's Day Harlequin brings you all the essentials—romance, chocolate and jewelry—in:

VALENTINE Delights

Matchmaking chocolate-shop owner Papa Valentine dispenses sinful desserts, mouth-watering chocolates...and advice to the lovelorn, in this collection of three delightfully romantic stories by Meryl Sawyer, Kate Hoffmann and Gina Wilkins.

As our special Valentine's Day gift to you, each copy of *Valentine Delights* will have a beautiful, filigreed, heart-shaped brooch attached to the cover.

Make this your most delicious Valentine's Day ever with *Valentine Delights*!

Available in February wherever Harlequin books are sold.

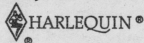

HARLEQUIN ®
®

Look us up on-line at: http://www.romance.net

VAL97

HARLEQUIN PRESENTS®

Watch for the latest story
in our exciting series:

FROM HERE
TO PATERNITY

when men find their way to fatherhood by fair means,
by foul or even by default!

Dominic had made it clear that he held Sophie
and baby Ryan responsible for ruining his life!

So why was he asking her to marry him?

#1873 DOMINIC'S CHILD
by
Catherine Spencer

Available in March wherever
Harlequin books are sold.

Jake wasn't sure why he'd agreed to take the place
of his twin brother, nor why he'd agreed to commit
Nathan's crime. Maybe it was misplaced loyalty.

DANGEROUS
Temptation

by *New York Times* bestselling author

Anne MATHER

After surviving a plane crash, Jake wakes up in a hospital
room and can't remember anything—or anyone...
including one very beautiful woman who comes to see
him. His wife. Caitlin. Who watches him so guardedly.

Her husband seems like a stranger to Caitlin—he's full of
warmth and passion. Just like the man she thought she'd
married. Until his memory returns. And with it, a danger
that threatens them all.

Available in February 1997 at your favorite retail outlet.

MIRA The brightest star in women's fiction   MAMDT

HARLEQUIN PRESENTS®

**They say it's the quiet ones
you have to watch...**

Isobel a temptress?
Patrick couldn't believe it—she seemed
so modest, so reserved.

But then he, too, began to fall under her spell...

Find out more in Anne Mather's new story
#1869 WICKED CAPRICE

Available in March wherever
Harlequin books are sold.

HARLEQUIN®

Don't miss these Harlequin favorites by some of our most distinguished authors!
And now, you can receive a discount by ordering two or more titles!

HT#25645	THREE GROOMS AND A WIFE by JoAnn Ross	$3.25 U.S. ☐
		$3.75 CAN. ☐
HT#25647	NOT THIS GUY by Glenda Sanders	$3.25 U.S. ☐
		$3.75 CAN. ☐
HP#11725	THE WRONG KIND OF WIFE by Roberta Leigh	$3.25 U.S. ☐
		$3.75 CAN. ☐
HP#11755	TIGER EYES by Robyn Donald	$3.25 U.S. ☐
		$3.75 CAN. ☐
HR#03416	A WIFE IN WAITING by Jessica Steele	$3.25 U.S. ☐
		$3.75 CAN. ☐
HR#03419	KIT AND THE COWBOY by Rebecca Winters	$3.25 U.S. ☐
		$3.75 CAN. ☐
HS#70622	KIM & THE COWBOY by Margot Dalton	$3.50 U.S. ☐
		$3.99 CAN. ☐
HS#70642	MONDAY'S CHILD by Janice Kaiser	$3.75 U.S. ☐
		$4.25 CAN. ☐
HI#22342	BABY VS. THE BAR by M.J. Rodgers	$3.50 U.S. ☐
		$3.99 CAN. ☐
HI#22382	SEE ME IN YOUR DREAMS by Patricia Rosemoor	$3.75 U.S. ☐
		$4.25 CAN. ☐
HAR#16538	KISSED BY THE SEA by Rebecca Flanders	$3.50 U.S. ☐
		$3.99 CAN. ☐
HAR#16603	MOMMY ON BOARD by Muriel Jensen	$3.50 U.S. ☐
		$3.99 CAN. ☐
HH#28885	DESERT ROGUE by Erine Yorke	$4.50 U.S. ☐
		$4.99 CAN. ☐
HH#28911	THE NORMAN'S HEART by Margaret Moore	$4.50 U.S. ☐
		$4.99 CAN. ☐

(limited quantities available on certain titles)

	AMOUNT	$
DEDUCT:	10% DISCOUNT FOR 2+ BOOKS	$
ADD:	POSTAGE & HANDLING	$
	($1.00 for one book, 50¢ for each additional)	
	APPLICABLE TAXES*	$_____
	TOTAL PAYABLE	$_____
	(check or money order—please do not send cash)	

To order, complete this form and send it, along with a check or money order for the total above, payable to Harlequin Books, to: **In the U.S.:** 3010 Walden Avenue, P.O. Box 9047, Buffalo, NY 14269-9047; **In Canada:** P.O. Box 613, Fort Erie, Ontario, L2A 5X3.

Name: _____

Address: _____ City: _____

State/Prov.: _____ Zip/Postal Code: _____

*New York residents remit applicable sales taxes.
 Canadian residents remit applicable GST and provincial taxes.
Look us up on-line at: http://www.romance.net

HBACK-JM4